"I'm glad you did come," he whispered.

"Even though I'm as conflicted as hell about this, I wanted to see you again—almost from the moment I left you. When I say that I can't get involved with you, that's the truth. I can't. But that doesn't mean I don't want to."

He smiled, then leaned forward and kissed the back of her hand. "So will you forgive me for hurting you? Because I'd rather crack another rib than do that."

Solaina drew in a ragged breath. She was leaving; David was staying. So there was no destiny involved here, and she simply had to keep her head about that.

"David, this—"

Before her words were out, he stood up and pulled her into his arms. There, locked in his embrace, battling with surrender and yet still contemplating retreat, she felt his lips on hers in shock—not so much because she hadn't expected the kiss, but because she hadn't known how much she wanted it.

Dear Reader

Welcome to my third medical romance!

Every time I sit down to create one of these stories I dig deep into my medical experiences to see if there's something, or someone, who might be my inspiration—and every time I go right back to my grandmother. She was an extraordinary nurse, who started out as a floor-sweeper in a small-town medical practice and worked her way through education and rank to achieve great things in her career.

In this story, my character Solaina finds herself in a position for which she clearly does not feel she is qualified—much like my grandmother did. One day, Grandma was literally asked to put down her broom and assist in a surgery. This was her first ever brush with patient care in any capacity, and also the day that changed her life for ever. Certainly she doubted herself at that moment. Who wouldn't? But she met the challenge and triumphed.

In life, we're all faced with challenges. Most won't be as drastic as my grandmother's—from floor-sweeper to surgical nurse in the blink of an eye. Some may be, however. It's my wish for you that as these challenges come to you you're able to use them, as Solaina and my grandmother did, to help move you in a new and exciting direction in your life, and triumph!

Wishing you health and happiness!

Dianne Drake

PS—Solaina has a twin sister, Solange. Look for her upcoming story in THE DOCTOR'S COURAGEOUS BRIDE.

24:7

**The cutting edge of
Mills & Boon® Medical Romance™**

The emotion is deep
The drama is real
The intensity is fierce

CHAPTER ONE

NIGHTTIME. When had that happened? David Gentry raised himself up on an elbow and swatted at the mosquito buzzing around his face. It was the size of a hummingbird. He'd been lying out here in the jungle for who knew how long, sleeping. Or more likely unconscious. The mosquitoes could have feasted off him for hours by now. Maybe days, since he had no idea how long he'd been there.

He took a swing at another blood-sucking predator. Surely he must have had a malaria shot, but he didn't know. In fact, all he knew right now was his name, and he wasn't sure enough about that to wager on it.

He moved to sit up, winced, then went back to reclining, propped up one one elbow. Now it was coming back in pieces. Someone kicking him…the crack of his bones. That's something he did remember. Two or three ribs, he decided as he probed the tender area. Left side, and he would definitely wager on the bruise there, even though he couldn't see it in the dark. But he felt it—soreness starting just under his shoulder and stopping just above his waist. There were probably three or four broken ribs, judging from the feel of it.

He tried to get up. Easier said than done. His shoulder

hurt, too. The sting of it was only just now fighting its way through the pain of his ribs. It was either get up, or stay down, maybe for ever. David sat up, moving cautiously for fear he might puncture a lung on a jagged bone edge.

Good. He finally remembered something useful. Broken ribs could equal punctured lung could equal death. "A punctured lung and me without a chest tube," he grunted, making it to a full sitting position.

Just sitting there on the damp ground hurt worse than he'd thought pain could ever hurt. He dragged his forearm across his face to wipe away the sweat. "So what's a few broken ribs and a bullethole?"

Gingerly, David prodded his shoulder just to make sure the wound was real and not another delusion. And there it was. A sticky mess. A painful, sticky mess. "That's why you've got the fever, Davey," he said, wiping his brow again. The ooze of infection in his shoulder from the bullet was probably the worst thing going on inside him right now, and if he didn't get it treated soon… Unless one of his ribs had stabbed him through the lung. Then either way—infection or collapsed lung—it wouldn't matter. He'd be dead.

And the call of the damp ground below him was getting louder. Just another hour, Davey. One more hour then you'll feel well enough to get up and walk out of here.

Another hour's sleep did sound good. Just one…

Still sitting upright, he was just too tired now to go all the way back down to the ground. Wasted effort, really, for a short nap. His eyes started to flutter closed, and he let out a long, exhausted sigh. Maybe he would sink back down after all. The ground wasn't so hard. Nice patches of moss… Just an hour…

But he wanted a drink first. A sip of water then off to bed with him! Goodnight, sleep tight, don't let the bedbugs bite! He reached over to his bedside stand to grab a glass…but the only thing his hand clamped hold of was a heap of soggy leaves. Immediately, David snapped his eyes open, trying to hold onto the little bit of reality he had left to him. Sleep meant sure death this time. It didn't take a doctor to figure out that he was too weak, too dehydrated, too infected to last the night.

It was a prognosis any first-year medical student could make. And at thirty-six, he was, what? Sixteen years past his first year of medical school? He tried to remember, tried to figure the simple math, but his head was too fuzzy to think.

David looked up at the canopy of palms and bamboos. By the light of the moon he could see the shadows, if not the actual trees. An evergreen forest. That, he could remember. Back home in Toronto, the trees in his mother's yard were deciduous. Another stupid thing to remember. Only a delirious man would sit here classifying trees, he thought, laughing out loud. "And if there are any of you tree snakes up there in those evergreen trees, you stay away from me, you hear? Mosquitoes are enough." Were there any vaccinations against tree snakes? He couldn't remember.

"OK, Davey, you've got to do better than this if you want to get yourself out of here. So quit talking to the snakes." Cobras and kraits and vipers. All deadly.

He looked up again, imagining all kinds of glowing eyes looking back at him. "Focus, Davey. That's the only way you're going to make it out of here." But on what? He didn't have anything in reserve. Not even an ounce of strength left to muster.

Something rustled in the brush next to him, and he turned

to see what was there. Like he could see anything in the dark. Your head going wonky again, he thought. Or a snake.

The thought caused him to shudder, which set off a round of pain shooting from his ribs straight through to his brain. He clamped his arm over his rib cage to support it.

"Get it together, Davey," he warned himself once the initial rip of the pain was over. "Now, or never." He glanced sideways at the brush next to him. Maybe if he could just grab hold of something, he might be able to pull himself to his feet… Mosses, orchids, ferns. No pulling power in those. Even though it was dark and he couldn't see what was surrounding him, he had a vague recollection of what he'd seen before he'd gone fuzzy the last time, and nothing he could dredge up from his bleariness was sufficient to grab hold of. He had to focus on this or he'd lie right back down and die.

And David surely did not want to die. Not here. Not now. Not like this. He'd walked so many miles in this condition because he wanted to live, and that was something simple he could remember.

"Damn," he muttered, trying to wipe out the image of his own death. "So find a rhododendron bush, Davey. That'll do it." Big, woody, deep roots—grabbing onto a rhododendron might work. They were all over the place, low-lying under the trees, thriving in the shade. He should be able to pull himself up if he had the strength to hold on. If he had the strength to hoist his entire body weight. If he had the strength to walk once he was upright.

David looked up again to make sure those glowing eyes weren't getting closer. Never mind the ground predators. Monkeys he could deal with. Even the deer and the kouprey. But now he was imagining wild dogs and tigers and rhinos.

Worst of all, bats. He'd just as soon meet a tiger as a bat. And the bats in Dharavaj were almost as big as the tigers.

He was back in Dharavaj, wasn't he? Not in Cambodia any more?

"Time to assess. The doctor needs water." He ran his dry tongue over his cracked lips, emphasizing just how much. "And the doctor needs antibiotics." His scorching forehead was the testament to that. He didn't have to touch it to feel just how feverish it was. He knew. "But most of all, the doctor needs to get out of here." If that happened, and if, by some miracle, he did make it back to his little clinic outside Kantha, he might stand a fighting chance of recovery.

Of course, he could simply lie back down and wait until daylight and hope to wake up again. Yes, that was it. Sleep for the remainder of the night and start all over again in the morning. Seeing how to get home would be so much easier.

David sank back to the damp ground, his head resting on a pillow of moss, and shut his eyes. "Until morning," he murmured wearily, as the dark cloud of oblivion started to roll back over him once more. "Only until morning." He heaved a deep sigh, pleased with the decision.

"Morning…" In the morning he would… He didn't remember. Couldn't remember. Surgery? Did someone need surgery? He thought so, but he couldn't find his work schedule. Another amputation. Another patient on the brink of death! That was it. But who?

The name wouldn't come up out of the depths, and he couldn't sleep until he remembered. "Think, Davey…" He could almost see his little operating room. And, yes, that was him standing over the operating table. But who was on the table? He still couldn't tell…

"Don't start the procedure until you verify the patient," he warned himself.

But he was starting anyway, because his patient was dying, and he had to do something to save him. Right now! The scalpel was in his hand, and he was pulling back the sheet to make the first cut.

The sheet finally came off the patient's face.

"No!" he choked, looking down at himself. He was the patient!

Suddenly, David's eyes popped open and he struggled into a sitting position. Out of breath, he reached out into the dark for an handhold that would help him to his feet. And he found it. A bush, mere inches away. Maybe a rhododendron, maybe not. He couldn't tell from the feel of it, didn't know if it would be his saving grace tonight. Or his last, failing hope.

He steadied himself then pulled, and his first effort raised him mere inches off the ground. "Gotta do this another way," he grunted, realizing how much the next try was going to hurt. Getting himself over on his knees meant putting weight on the shoulder where the bullet was lodged. If he failed, and if he fell back down face first, he risked driving one of those broken ribs right through his lung.

Resetting himself for his second try, David gritted his teeth to the pain as he turned over and positioned himself on his hands and knees. If not for the fact that he was already so dehydrated, he would have been sweating much more than he was. Sweating profusely and shaking. He worked his hand through the branches to find the biggest. Everything, so far, was spindly. Too spindly. Like the way his legs felt.

He found a handhold. Nice, thick, sturdy…and it slipped right thought his sweaty, shaky hand.

It was early June, the height of the hot season, and though the temperature was probably climbing up to 38 degrees Celsius now, the rest of his shaking was coming from the chill that results of a spiked fever and infection. And exposure. His body systems were shutting down, and confused over how to go about doing that. He was hot, he was cold, he was delirious, he was rational. It didn't matter which of those came to pass now because they all felt the same. Miserable.

David took hold of a sturdy branch, shut his eyes tight, forcing himself to concentrate on holding on. Then he dragged in a deep, ragged breath, and pulled, screaming at the top of his lungs and expelling all his reserved oxygen as he pulled himself up. Inch by agonizing inch, he ascended, pulling tighter and tighter on the bush until, amazing, he was there. He was upright, and it surprised him because his two jelly-like legs held him up.

"Good job," he panted, trying to figure out the next part of his plan. Get up and…and, what? That's as far as he'd gone. So, get up and…stay up. That was it. Easily enough said, and actually easier done than he'd anticipated, as he pulled himself through the bush to the first tree he found. Then he hugged that tree like he'd never hugged anything, or anyone, before. Simply hugged it. He threw his arms around it like it was a the most beautiful woman he'd ever seen…

He had seen her once. Not his delusion. Stunning. Black hair, dark eyes. And he was holding onto her now until the wobbling in his knees subsided, the spinning in his head slowed down and he was able to draw normal breath again. She needed an orchid in her hair.

"OK," he said to the treetrunk, squeezing her out and reality back in. "Now, let's see what we can do about getting out of here." Pulling back from the tree, he took a few steps, and another few steps, one at a time, until his legs were back under him. In the dark, in an area he didn't know, he had absolutely no idea which way to go to get out. But it didn't matter. This would have been the place he would have died tonight, and anyplace else was better than there.

It was later than usual, and Solaina didn't like driving this stretch of road after dark. She made the drive every weekend, from her apartment in Chandella to the nice little seaside cottage she rented down south, near the national park. White sands, blue waters—this was what she thought about all week long. But today the meeting had run long, and her departure had been delayed.

Normally, Solaina Léandre enjoyed the winding drive. Often, she would see the profusion of gaily colored beach umbrellas in the public areas—belonging to residents of Dharavaj who lived in the cities and escaped there to the shore as she did. It wasn't a prominent tourist area largely owing to the fact that it was still undiscovered by most of the world. Just a sleepy little strip of a country where the towns and cities were scattered so far apart, travel from place to place was inconvenient. Because tourists wanted convenience, they didn't come to Dharavaj, which, as far as Solaina was concerned, made Dharavaj perfect.

Sometimes as she traveled down from Chandella, then out onto the little peninsula where her cottage was nestled into the beach, she would stop to watch the heads of swimmers bobbing up and down in the surf, or the picnickers enjoying a festive spread of local fruits and sweets from their hampers.

Once, she had stopped to observe some grave markers. All along this stretch was a favorite place for Chandella's Chinese to bury their dead. It wasn't a cemetery in the traditional sense since Dharavaj was largely Buddhist and there were no cemeteries. But rather this stretch was the place where loved ones picked out a beautiful spot along the roadside, preferably one with an ocean view. *What better way to spend eternity*, she thought, *looking out over all of this?*

Except tonight she wasn't looking out over anything. It was late, she was tired, and she was dreaming of bed. In fact, her eyes were fighting to drop shut right now, after a couple hours of driving, and she was losing the battle. She wondered whether she should pull over and take a nap, after cranking up the volume on the CD player hadn't done the trick. The Berlioz *Symphonie Fantastique* really should have popped her eyes right back open, but tonight even Hector's best efforts weren't good enough.

Ten minutes away from her little cottage, and it was getting so difficult. "Wake up, Solaina. You really don't want to pull over and shut it down. Too hot out there. Too much humidity." Without the air-conditioning running, she wasn't sure she'd survive five minutes in the car, let alone an hour for a quick nap.

"So, just wake up! Keep your eyes open, and focus on the road. That's all you have to do. Focus." She forced her eyes open even wider, feeling a little better. It made sense, talking to herself. "Good idea." There was no one out here at this time of the night to look questioningly into her car and pronounce her crazy. "So why not?" she said. "Talk. Tell me all your hopes and dreams."

Hopes and dreams? "I want to get to the cottage. That's my hope. And my dream is that the air-conditioning is working. Next question?"

She thought for a minute, going back to her earlier conversation with Solange, her twin sister. "So tell me, what is it you're really looking for in a man?" Solange had asked, sounding much too much like a nosy television reporter.

Tough question, though, because she'd never really put together a real composite. Most of the time the men in her life came as whoever was convenient. One or two dates, nothing serious, nothing interesting, then she walked away. It was safer that way. The circuit of her life, and she wouldn't accidentally end up with someone like her mother had. She shuddered at the thought. "Well, handsome wouldn't be bad." Good place to start. Scandinavian could be interesting. "Blue eyes. Make that ice blue. Definitely ice blue. And piercing." She nodded, pleased with that. "OK, so this one's blond, with blue eyes. I also want lots of muscles. Big man. Broad chest…" Another nice image she was pleased with. As Solaina thought about her perfect man, her mind drifted off just a bit.

Then suddenly a moving image caught her attention, just off to the side of her headlights, and before she could snap her attention back fully, she heard a thud off her left fender. Immediately, she felt a sick knot in the pit of her stomach, and by the time she got the car stopped, she wondered if she might have run into a deer, or a kouprey, which was, essentially, a wild cow.

She wrestled with the idea of getting out of her car to take a look. Alone, after dark, nowhere…not a good idea. If it was an animal, as much as the thought of even that made her sick to her stomach, there was no need to get out. And who, in their right mind, would be wandering around out here anyway? Nobody. There were no little villages, and the resorts were long behind her. No tribal areas—most of the tribespeople stuck to the interior. So it had to be an animal, right?

Solaina looked into her rear-view mirror and all she could

see was black. "An animal," she said, as she opened her window. "Anybody back there?" she yelled. "Are you hurt?"

She listened, but there was no response.

"Anybody there? Did I hurt you?"

Again, no response. So Solaina rolled up the window and set the auto in forward and started to go, only to come to a rolling stop a few inches further on, throw open her car door, and get out. "OK. I'm coming back, and you'd better not try anything funny because…" She had nothing to finish off that threat, so she headed back to the point of impact, fully expecting to find some poor creature sprawled there. "Hell, I hope it's not suffering," she said, as she crept along. She was an animal lover, a tree lover, a bug lover. She was the one who, as a child, would run outside after a rainstorm and gather all the earthworms that had wiggled out of the ground then put them back so nobody would step on them. Or, worse, before the sun came out and dried them out. "Hello," she called out into the night. "Is somebody out there?"

She paused, listening. Something close by was stirring. She could hear it. Was that a moan?

"Hello," she whispered, not quite brave enough now to call out.

"Hello," someone whispered back,

Solaina jumped, stifling a scream, and her heart doubled its rhythm, slamming into her chest wall. "Are you hurt?" she ventured, creeping slowly forward, wondering now if this was the wisest thing to be doing on an isolated road in the middle of the night. In the middle of nowhere.

Maybe she should have gone on to the cottage and called someone. But who? She didn't know anybody around here. She hardly even knew anybody in Dharavaj, aside from her co-workers, and she'd been here two years. Howard and Victoria? No, they were off on an elephant adventure in the north country somewhere. No ambulance service out here, no policemen. Nobody to call. And this was her doing after all. She'd been the one who'd run him down, so she'd have to be the one off to his rescue.

Solaina dragged in a deep breath, and continued creeping forward in the direction from which the man's weak hello had come, hoping this was just her mind playing tricks on her. A strange voice in the night, on a deserted roadside, was a typical gothic scene in a horror movie. It's what her mind expected from this. That's all.

"I'm hurt," he sputtered. "Dying, I think."

Judging from his accent, he was American, or Canadian perhaps. "Where are you?" she ventured, still creeping on.

He didn't answer.

"Hello? Can you talk to me?"

No answer again, and now she was getting worried. He'd either succumbed, or maybe he was a mugger trying to lure her in. So she hesitated. "I need you hear your voice so I can find you. You've got to talk to me if you want me to help you." Creeping around in the dark like she was, with only the stationary light of her car beams to help, she could be standing right next to him and not even see him.

"Where you come from, do you have deciduous trees?" he finally asked, his voice so weak she thought she hadn't heard him correctly.

"What?" she asked, approaching the patch of bushes from where she thought she'd heard his voice.

"Deciduous trees. Do you have them?"

Yes, she'd heard him right the first time. A strange question, but nevertheless a valuable one because it led Solaina right to the spot when he was sprawled flat on the ground. "We have both deciduous and evergreen," she said, bending over him and suddenly wishing she had better nursing skills—practical skills, the kind that saved lives. Because even in the little bit of light she had, this man looked to her like he truly was about to die. Soon!

CHAPTER TWO

"You've got a good pulse," she said, her fingers still in place along the side of his neck. Good pulse, and much stronger than she'd expected from her first look at him. "Which means you must be a pretty strong man." Strong, with a will to live. Thank God.

As she pulled her fingers away from the pulse point in his neck, Solaina felt the stickiness on her fingers, and instinctively raised them to her nose. That familiar coppery smell. Even though she rarely ever got near a bleeding patient these days, she knew this. Blood! He was bleeding, but she didn't think it was profusely. Not from what she could see in the dim headlamps of the car, anyway.

"Broken ribs," he gasped. "Left side. Fourth and fifth, and probably sixth. Maybe seventh. That one could be a tear to the intercostal cartilage."

So he's medical, she thought. Maybe a doctor? *Physician, I hope you can heal yourself because this nurse cannot.* "I think you're bleeding, too." What a pathetic response to a man who was already outclassing her as a medic, even after she'd run him down and nearly killed him.

"Shoulder," he moaned.

She'd broken his ribs and his shoulder? "I'm so sorry about this," Solaina gasped, pulling back his shirt to reveal his shoulder wound. "I didn't see you. I promise, I didn't see you anywhere." Of course, she'd been drowsy, and she was already cursing herself for being so stupid as to drive in that condition.

"But I saw you…" He coughed, then swore softly under his breath.

"Don't try to talk," she said. "You need to conserve your strength for getting out of here." However that was going to be accomplished. "Why couldn't you have run into the road in the middle of Chandella where there's real help?"

"Saw your headlights," he said.

Of course he had. He'd seen her headlights coming straight at him and there had been no time to jump away. Poor man. Solaina was already beginning to feel the sting of self-recrimination. She shouldn't have come here tonight. Not so late. Not when she'd been so tired. "Look, you really need to stay still for now." *Until I can figure out what to do.* "Until I can get you some help. So just concentrate on breathing, and staying awake." Good advice if he had a head trauma, which he probably did. Concussion, most likely. That happened when getting knocked about by a moving vehicle. *Her moving vehicle.* Just thinking that made her go nauseous.

"You're my help," he murmured.

Solaina laughed bitterly. "If only you knew how wrong you were about that." Even now, after ten years, there were so many nights when she tried to sleep and still saw Jacob Renner's face when she closed her eyes. He'd thought she'd been his help, too. "But I suppose that for now it is me, isn't it?" Another thought to add to her rising nausea.

Never let them hear the doubt—something she stressed to

her nurses. No matter what the situation, the patient was never to hear doubt, and right now she was praying that he couldn't hear the dubious tone in her words. "So the first thing, after I make sure that you can travel, is to decide where we're going."

She took a deep breath. *Checklist, Laina. He's breathing. He's conscious. He's somewhat lucid. All good signs. But he's bleeding. He has broken ribs, meaning he could puncture a lung.* She wouldn't have a clue how to save him from that! Book smarts, yes. She knew the theory. But in practice...

Pray God that he can get up and walk to my car. "OK. I'm going to do a quick look to see what else is wrong, other than the obvious. Any particular aches?"

"Plenty," he grunted, then sucked in a sharp breath as she probed his shoulder. "Does pride count?"

In spite of the situation, she had to laugh. "When you're healed, yes. It can count all you want it to. Right now, though, I want the real aches."

"My pride is a real ache."

Good sense of humor. *Stubborn.* Strong-willed. Not a bad combination, really. "Well, I can't probe your pride, so instead, I''m going to slide my fingers in under your neck to make sure there isn't any apparent neck damage. So, don't move your head."

She wriggled her fingers carefully between his neck and the dirt. An initial probe found nothing to the touch. No open wounds, no dried blood. "Good," she murmured.

"Oh," he moaned. "A little lower..."

"Pain?" she asked. "Can you tell me exactly where it is?"

"Massage..."

She pulled her hand away from his neck. "Not a massage."

She chuckled. The tension knot in her neck could certainly stand a massage, though.

"Later, pretty lady. I promise."

"Let's hope that later you're in a proper hospital bed, well on your way to recovery." She eased her fingers to his shoulder wound. Old blood there. Congealed. Clumped. Crusted. "How long ago did this shoulder wound happen?" she asked, sure now that it was an old wound, and not one of her causing.

"Don't know. Two days…three…" His voice trailed off.

"Don't fade out on me," she said, feeling for any signs of fresh bleeding. There didn't seem to be any. "I need to know what kind of wound this is." It was small, compact. To her fingers, it seemed a puncture of some sort, or a gunshot wound. Judging from the feel of it, the wound might already be healing over, but the surrounding tissue was ablaze. Meaning infection.

"Take me home," he wheezed.

Delirious again. From the infection, most likely. Solaina laid the back of her hand across his brow. "You're burning up," she said, almost stunned. His temperature was well over normal. Maybe by as much as five or six degrees, she estimated. "And dehydrated, I'm guessing." To make sure, she brushed her fingers over his face and felt his dried, cracked lips.

"I always knew it would feel good when you did that."

"This isn't a date." She laughed, checking his neck again for a pulse. Still strong. He was still strong, and apparently a bit randy. That, she knew, could come with a head injury.

"I meant to ask you."

"I'm sure you did."

"But you didn't see me."

No, she hadn't seen him on the road. But she'd heard the sickening thump when she'd hit him. Just thinking about that caused the nausea roiling around in her belly to give her another whack. "I'm so sorry," she whispered, trying to fight off the memory of that sound. He had been wandering around out there in the night, along the road, already injured, and she'd run him down.

"Gunshot," he murmured.

"What?"

"Got shot."

The shoulder wound! That made sense, judging from the feel of his shoulder. Of course, she'd never treated a GSW, except as a student. And then she'd only observed from the back of the cluster of other student nurses, and had eventually been the one who had been singled out to put on the dressing. A lousy dressing! That was her total experience in this.

"Well, you're in luck because I do have some rather unique experience in the treatment of gunshot wounds," she said. Above all else, keep the patient confident in you. Another thing she told her nurses.

"No exit," he whispered.

His voice was weaker now. Weaker and wobbly. "Shh," she said, slipping her hand under his shoulder to assess the area. "You just stay quiet, and let me take care of you. Did I tell you that I'm a nurse?" By professional standards, anyway. Although not by her own. So claiming nurse, under these circumstances, was like saying, *Did I tell you I'm a hairstylist?* or *Did I tell you that I'm a gardener?* The hairstylist and the gardener stood as good a chance of aiding him as she did. Maybe better, since they didn't have a near-pathological fear.

"Did I tell you that I love nurses?"

"All right, Casanova. I've got to have a look at the back of your shoulder. So don't move." The area at the back of his shoulder was intact. No torn flesh, no bleeding. So, he was correct. There was no exit wound. The bullet was still in there. And if he'd been stumbling about in the dirt, all sweaty… She shuddered, thinking about the grime and filthy bits he might have festering inside his wound. After a few days, it couldn't be good at all. He was one lucky man to be alive in any condition, having blood loss and all his other injuries on top of a dirty, purulent wound. So many possibilities. Infection, pneumonia…

"Take a deep breath for me, will you?" she asked, wondering about the extent of his rib injuries. Had he constricted his breathing so much that pneumonia could be setting in already?

"It hurts."

"I'm sure it does, but I need to have a listen to your lungs, and the only way I can do that is if you take a nice, deep breath for me."

"My lungs are fine," he argued.

"Then let me have a listen, and if they are, I'll be the one to tell you, instead of the other way around." She wished she had a stethoscope, because an ear to the chest wasn't going to tell her much. But she didn't. So, after she'd unbuttoned his shirt all the way down, she pressed her ear to his chest and listened. Nice, strong heartbeat. So much so it was almost hypnotic. And a nice mat of soft hair, too. *Something she shouldn't be noticing.*

She held her own breath for a second, listening for fluid, then breathed out a sigh of relief. No audible sounds meant there was a pretty good chance he didn't have pneumonia. "Excellent," she said, straightening back up. "I didn't hear anything."

"You can listen again," he said. "Your hair smells nice."

Self-consciously, Solaina reached up and ran her fingers

through her hair. It was down. The pins that usually kept it up gone. "I've got to unzip your pants now," she said, pushing her hair back from her face. "Evaluate your belly for rigidity or tenderness, to see if you have…" No point in telling him. If he was truly medical, he knew she would be looking for signs of internal bleeding. If he was not medical, there was no reason to scare him. Though, amazingly, he didn't seem scared. Not at all.

"I don't like bats. Don't mind tigers, but I don't like bats."

Not scared, but apparently in delirium again. Solaina smiled. So many truths slipped out in delirium, deep dark secrets and long-hidden personality traits. "I don't mind them so much," she said, pulling his jeans down below his waist, then probing his stomach for any obvious wound—obvious to the touch, since in the dimness of the headlights she couldn't see much.

Nice stomach. Hard, flat. And, thank heavens, not rigid from an internal injury. This man was getting luckier by the minute. "Bats eat the mosquitoes, which are so much worse out here than the bats. So I think the bats are fine."

She really needed a better look overall. But before she moved him, or before she even tried getting him into her auto, she did want to have a more complete idea of what she was dealing with. "Look, I'll be right back," she said. "I'm going to pull my car up closer and turn the beams straight onto us. So you stay here. Don't move. Don't get up." As if he could.

It took only a minute before Solaina was back at his side, this time in the full glare of her car headlights. As she bent down next to him and got her first good look, she saw that he was handsome. Handsome underneath an awful lot of dirt, and covered with dried blood and particles and pieces of the jungle. "Are you awake?" she asked, deciding that instead of zipping up his jeans she was going to remove them to make sure he had no serious leg injuries. He might, and in his condition he wouldn't even know it.

"Take away the scalpel," he said. "I don't want it. Not yet."

"Trust me. Nobody in their right mind would let me go near a scalpel." Before the jeans came off, Solaina removed his shoes and socks, and saw that his feet looked good. No evident injuries. Then she pulled down the jeans, and set about an exam of his legs, first the right, then the left. There were so many bruises, she noted, almost as horrified by that as by anything else she'd seen. No fractures that she could tell as she ran her hands from his hip bones to his ankles on both sides. But dozens and dozens of bruises, large and small. And not fresh.

This man had certainly taken a beating and, as best as she could tell in the light from the car, they were taking on the greenish-yellow hue of being several days old. Something quite noticeable on a fair-skinned man, as he was.

Suddenly, Solaina looked at his hair. Blond? It was so dirty she couldn't really tell, but she thought he was. "This isn't how I wanted to meet my blond man," she said, lifting his right leg to make sure there were no horrible cuts on the back of it.

"Sandy," he said. "Not true blond."

"So you're with me right now?" Seeing nothing but bruises on his right leg, she took a look at the underside of his left, discovering only more bruises.

"For a minute, then I may have to go away again."

The man was astute. He knew his condition, knew what he was fighting against here. And he was struggling to stay with her. That was good, because until she could get him to help, *real help,* the only thing he had going for him was a strong will. Certainly, that was much better than her paltry skills in a situation like this. "OK, so while you're with me, can you tell me your name?"

"David. David Gentry."

Solaina gasped. She'd heard his name almost a year ago, in Cambodia, when she'd sent a couple of her nurses off to have a go with IMO—International Medical Outreach. He had been a lead doctor with IMO at the time—an amazing orthopaedic surgeon, everyone had said. But he'd walked away from it all. No reason. At least none that she'd heard. "David Gentry," Solaina repeated. "Are you Dr David Gentry?"

"When I'm not delirious I am. Can't say for sure the rest of the time."

"So can you tell me what happened to you, David? Other than the fact that I ran over you?"

"You didn't. I did."

"What?"

"I ran into you. Saw your headlights. Needed help, or die right there." He sucked in a tattered, shallow breath. "Glad it was you because I've always thought you were the most beautiful woman I've ever seen."

Nice compliment, as delirious compliments went. But he was delirious again, and she needed to get him some help.

Solaina took his pulse one more time, then sucked in her own tattered breath. "Don't know how I'm going to do this, Doctor, but I'm going to get you out of here now." After that? She didn't have a clue.

"That will do, I think," Solaina said, as she fashioned one leg of his jeans around his chest to support his broken ribs. A few snips, a couple of tucks and, *voilà*, instant brace. Satisfactory for now. Even though she didn't have any great medical equipment tucked into a handy medical bag, Solaina was grateful for the first-aid kit she kept in her car, because the adhesive tape worked brilliantly to tape that makeshift brace into place. Rather ingenious, she thought, rocking back on her heels to appraise her work. The denim was a nice sturdy fabric. It had give, but it also had strength. Give and take, which was exactly what David needed until she could get him some X-rays and a professional wrap job.

Of course, he was an orthopedist. He would be the best one to do what he desperately needed done, and here she was, doing the doctoring. "Are you able to breathe?" Solaina asked, slipping her fingers under the wrap to make sure she hadn't taped it too tightly in place.

"I was until I saw you. And now all I want to do is find an orchid for your hair."

Solaina repositioned herself next to David to start the process of getting him up, wondering if, in his right mind, he was a romantic. He could be, with all his delusional references. "Well, Casanova, orchid or not, I've got to figure out how to get you up." This was going to be a struggle, and he wasn't going to be much help. Especially now that he was slipping back into delirium.

"Your orchid, Is it over your right or your left ear?" he asked.

"That's Hawaiian, Doctor." An orchid over the left ear meant married. Over the right meant single. Without thinking, Solaina reached up and brushed the hair back from her right ear, as David reached up and touched her left.

"That's good," he said, his hand dropping right back to the ground. "No orchid."

Even in his delirium he was fascinating. Charming. Appealing, in a down-and-out sort of way. *What would you be like when you're healthy, and all your mental faculties not quite so muzzy?* Somebody she would admire? Perhaps someone she'd like to get to know? "Let's talk about orchids another time. OK? Right now, we've got to concentrate on getting you up off the ground and into my car." Her very small car, unfortunately.

Asian cars were so small, which she actually liked because they were also efficient. Except right she wouldn't have minded one of those American behemoths, lots of metal, lots of gas and lots of room…room being the priority here because, as it turned out, David Gentry was quite a tall man. Much taller than she would have guessed from his sprawled-out form on the ground. "OK, David, I'm going to try lifting you. But you're going to have to help me." From a patient bed to standing she could do it, from the ground up she wasn't sure. "Arms around my neck, and when I give you the go, pull yourself up." He did, and the effort barely pulled him off the ground. It did manage to pull Solaina right over on top of him, which knocked him backwards into the dirt.

He moaned, grabbing for his ribs as she rolled off him. "You're heavy."

No one had ever accused her of that before. At five feet four inches, she had a small frame, and while she wasn't skinny, she wasn't heavy either. Of course, to David, a leaf fluttering down onto his broken ribs would feel heavy. She couldn't imagine what having her on top of them felt like. "Did I hurt you?" she gasped, plucking herself out of the dirt then immediately scrambling to his side to see if she had injured him.

"Not hurt," he managed. "But I sure could use a rhododendron."

Maybe not hurt, she thought, but definitely loopy again, and now, because his skirmish with dementia was coming and going so often, she was starting to wonder if he might have suffered more head trauma in his ordeal than she'd initially thought. A concussion? Maybe something worse, like a skull fracture? Head trauma of any kind scared her because out here there was no way to diagnose it, let alone do a little makeshift first aid on it like she'd done to his ribs. A wrap around his head made from the other leg of his jeans would do his head absolutely no good. Nothing she had would.

"I have a nice big rhododendron next to my cottage," Solaina replied. It was a bush. Maybe it was a rhododendron. She didn't know, didn't really care either. All she wanted to do was get him in her car, and if promising him a rhododendron was what it took, so be it. "Maybe you can have a look at it once I get you into the car and get you back there."

Her cottage was only ten minutes from here after all, the quickest place to take him, since he wasn't critical. Injured horribly, yes, but not critically. And the plan that was finally coming to mind was to get him back there, then clean him up and call Howard Brumley about what to do next. Maybe Howard knew a doctor around here who could take a look at David. Or, with some luck, there might a clinic somewhere nearby she didn't know about that Howard did.

Whatever the case, she didn't want to get Howard off his elephant excursion for good, merely long enough for a consult and a moral push, because she was already in way over her head.

Howard would have a solution for her. She was sure of that.

A melancholy smile crossed her lips, thinking about Howard. She would miss him desperately when she left

Chandella in a few weeks. In fact, she was missing him already, even before she'd left. Dr Howard Brumley. Her dear friend, and the absolute best doctor in the world. He would, without a doubt, have a solution for her about David Gentry. "So, any suggestions on how to get you from here to the car door?" It wasn't far. Quite close, in fact. Solaina calculated just a few giant steps but, oh, how imposing, when he couldn't walk and she certainly didn't have the strength to carry him.

"I can crawl," he said. "It's humiliating, but it works."

"Crawl as in on your hands and knees?" she asked. "What about your shoulder?" Crawling could open an already dangerous wound, and she wasn't sure she wanted to risk that. Out here, it was so easy for untreated dirty infections like his to turn gangrenous, and if David's infection was anywhere near that stage, there was a risk it would spread systemically.

Without answering, David turned over and crawled the few feet to her car. Then he collapsed alongside it, lying flat in the dirt, gazing upward. "So, what's next?" he panted.

"You just hop in the car, and I'll take you round to my cottage." If only it were that easy.

"And exactly what parts of me would you suggest hop?"

It was nice to have him back in his right mind. When he was that way, even under these dreadful circumstances, she felt better. Felt more confident. Felt more capable. "I think that right now I'd be happy to see any part of you hop into my car." She knelt down alongside David. "Now, arms around my neck."

"Didn't we try that already? I seem to recall you on top of me. Or was that a dream come true?"

Solaina chuckled. "You don't give up, do you, Casanova?"

"Where there's breath, there's hope."

"Well, take the breath and hold it, and let's see if we can

get you up enough to get you into my car seat." Bracing herself to his drag, Solaina did manage to get herself upright under his almost dead weight. At least enough to where he was able to fall backwards into the seat of her diminutive auto. Then he leaned sideways against the headrest on the back of the seat, trying to catch his breath.

It took her a moment to catch her own. "I didn't hurt you, did I?"

"Other than my pride…" He shook his head.

"Pride doesn't count on the side of the road in the middle of the night. Especially when you're not wearing pants. So now we've got to get your legs in," she said. They were so long, she wondered if that was possible.

"Nap first," he mumbled. "Then you can take care of my legs any way you like." With that, David's eyes shut and his head fell forward until his chin was resting on his chest. Immediately, he let out a little snore.

"I know you're exhausted, Casanova" Solaina said, "but you really can't quit on this until I get you all the way in." She shook him gently on his leg. "David, wake up. Do you hear me? Wake up. I need your help with this." He may be tired, but she'd had a long day, too, and she was also tired. And all during that day, her visions for the better part of her night had involved sleep, some light reading, then more sleep. Never had she pictured this, or anything remotely close to it—trying to stuff some rangy, roadside Lothario into her undersized car.

Solaina took a deep breath, regrouped, then came back at it. "Wake up, David. I can't do this without you." She took a quick feel of his pulse. A little fast, but steady enough. "David." She tried one more time, without success.

It appeared David was in for a long nap. "Probably for the

best," she said as she bent first his right leg and forced it inside, then his left. Before she shut the car door, she gave those legs one last going-over. Nice, muscular. He was some kind of an athlete, she guessed. One whose legs had been kicked, or beaten, over and over. "What kind of trouble have you gotten yourself into?" she asked, as she belted him into his seat then finally shut the car door. "What kind of trouble have you gotten yourself into that someone would hurt you so badly?"

And leave him for dead.

David wanted to open his eyes. He desperately wanted to take a look around him to see if he'd been dreaming all of this, or if it was real—if *she* was real. He remembered bits and pieces of his trek through the jungle. Falling, pulling himself back up. Falling again. Trying to find a strong enough bush to hold onto as he pulled himself up once more.

Those images were there, ingrained but quite fragmented. And none of them coming together in a full picture, except one, and she was the most beautiful woman he'd ever seen in his life. "I wanted it to be you," he murmured. "Dreamed you would come for me." That's all he'd dreamt. The beautiful Solaina.

Right now, in his dream, she was taking him to her home. He wanted to count on that, wanted to open his eyes and find that it was about to come true. But he couldn't. Not at the moment. His body hurt, his mind was playing tricks on him because even in his near-unconsciousness, her fragrance filled his head. It was everywhere—on him, around him, in his every breath. It was like flowers… He remembered the smell of flowers on her. Not an orchid, even though he somehow connected her to an orchid.

So jasmine, perhaps? She *would* have the scent of jasmine,

she was too beautiful not to. "Jasmine," he murmured. He was convinced of it now. Jasmine. "Just like the first time."

"I thought it was orchid. Or rhododendron."

A real voice? Or simply another part of his dream? He forced his eyes open a just a crack, but everything surrounding him was a mere blur. Was he in a car? A very small car? All crammed in with his knees practically up under his chin? *And without his pants?*

No, that couldn't be right. He wouldn't go anywhere without his pants.

David ran his hands over his legs, and felt nothing but flesh. Then he reached up and rubbed the makeshift bandage around his chest. It was all coming back to him now. "How long was I out?" he asked.

"Just a couple of minutes this time. But long enough that you didn't have to help get your legs into the car, which wasn't easy, by the way. How tall are you, David?"

"Six three," he answered, twisting to find a comfortable position.

"I wouldn't move too much if I were you," she cautioned. "I've got your ribs stabilized, and your shoulder's quit bleeding, so I don't want you causing any more problem to your injuries. We'll be at my cottage in another five minutes, and I promise you can take a good look at my rhododendron if you're so inclined."

"Why would I want to do that?" he asked, clearly puzzled.

Even though she didn't want to, Solaina laughed. "Something about rhododendrons and delirium, and deciduous trees. You've been in and out of it for the past fifteen minutes, babbling almost nonstop about the flora."

"Before that?" he asked.

"Before that, I didn't know you."

"But I dreamed about you before that."

"In the past fifteen minutes, you've gone in and out on me at least a half-dozen times. The mind has a funny way of distorting things when we're unconscious. I have seen people go unconscious for days and wake up believing it's only the next minute. Or people who have gone unconscious for seconds who wake up and recount these long, involved tales of what happened in their dream world during those brief moments. So, like I said, the mind has a funny way of distorting things, things that even the scientists can't explain like rhododendrons and orchids and deciduous trees."

"Do you wear jasmine?" he asked.

"I don't wear it, but my soap is jasmine."

David sighed and shut his eyes. It was time to return to his dream world, and he only hoped that she would be there in it with him. And with him when he woke up again. And now that he had found the lovely Solaina, he really did want to wake up again. Soon!

CHAPTER THREE

SOLAINA shut off the alarm clock and dragged herself out of the white rattan chair that was normally positioned across the room from her bed. Right now it was next to the bed, at an angle from which she could watch David breathe. Which was what she'd done for the past eight hours now. Inhalation. Exhalation. Inhale…exhale. In and out. One thing was sure. After fixing on it for so long, she definitely knew his pattern, knew when to expect a little snore from him or even a moan. She even knew the moments when he held onto his breath a little longer than he should have, because those first few times he'd done it she'd jumped up, expecting to have to revive him, only to discover that he didn't need it. He had been fine. Just breathing in his normal and what she decided was an exasperating pattern.

She'd called Howard the instant she'd stepped foot in the door. He had been off the elephant for the night and sipping cocktails in the hotel lounge, listening to a jazz quartet and smoking cigars. And now she was waiting, since Howard didn't drive at night. It seemed like days already, all cooped up and cranky there in her tiny cottage, with nothing but the sounds of David's breathing to listen to, and nothing but the rise and fall of his chest to watch. Then, of all things, trying to fix her breathing pattern to his.

There was ample room in there for one person, which was all that she'd wanted when she'd rented this little cozy-up well over a year ago. But now, with two people in it, and one of them so large, it was utterly overcrowded, practically bulging at the seams, and she could feel it closing in around her. Her uncluttered little arrangement with one single room sufficing for everything—bedroom, sitting room, kitchenette and dining cranny— was suddenly cluttered, and the more she thought about David being there, the smaller and tighter it was becoming.

And she wasn't, in the least, claustrophobic.

Solaina glanced over her lilliputian space, trying, for a moment, not to focus so much on David. It was a nice space, actually. There was no luxury, but she'd grown up with all the luxury money could buy, and she didn't need it any more. Didn't need it, didn't want it. Didn't particularly like it. Although with the nice salaries she'd earned in her positions over the years, along with an inheritance from her mother that was not yet touched, she could have afforded all the luxury she fancied. She just didn't fancy it.

And this little cottage, void of any extravagance, was just perfect, especially with its winding trail leading to the isolated stretch of beach just out her back door. With no neighbors close by, and no tourists on the undiscovered Dharavaj beaches, as far as she could see from the tiny bamboo terrace on which she spent most evenings here, this was the perfect place. Paradise. Shangri-la. It was what she craved. Her solitude.

Solaina took in a deep, relaxing breath and let the pristine peacefulness of it all wash its way through her. Yes, this little rental was the perfect place for her. Or for anyone who didn't wish to be bothered. And right now, fretting over this stranger was a bother. Especially since it was starting into the ninth hour since she'd dragged him inside, and she was faced with rousing herself from her chair every hour in order to give him a good, medical going-over. Howard's orders.

Eight hours done with, eight checks complete, and another hour and another check on the horizon. David was no better, no worse.

She couldn't say as much for herself, though.

Sometimes he stirred and asked bright questions of her. "What day is it, pretty lady? What time? Is it raining today?" Other times he was totally confused, mumbling on and on about flowers and bats and other gibberish. "I need that rho-dodendron! Get that bat out of here. Bring me an orchid."

Thank her smiling, red-lipped Buddha for Howard. After he'd told her there was no clinic nearby, or even a doctor, he'd given her medical instructions on David's care then promised to drive straight there with the morning light. She looked over at her little Buddha, the one that traveled everywhere with her. He was a bit of whimsy, with his fair skin and his big, red lips. He reclined on his side, his head propped in his hand, smil-ing and gazing up at the sky. Or maybe he was simply con-templating Nirvana. It was the way she wanted to live her life. Always gazing at the sky, always smiling, always happy. Contemplating Nirvana. She'd grown attached to this little souvenir because it was a reminder of the things she wanted.

That conversation with Howard had been so long ago now Solaina was almost ready to pace the floor, she was so edgy over the wait. And even her smiling Buddha wouldn't budge her mood.

"OK, so I cleaned the wound," she said, going over Howard's list for her for the fifth time. "I cleaned it, and I've gotten fluids down him." Even with her doctorate in nursing, all her administrative accolades, this was not her kind of nursing. And all she could think was, What if I made a mistake?

She directed a nursing department. Juggled schedules, met budgets, approved spending. But she didn't ever practice nursing in any fashion. Not where a patient was concerned. She was, most emphatically, *not* skilled in it, and she recognized her lack. Anything but the barest of patient care duties simply wasn't a risk she was willing to take. And, honestly, she didn't have any grand illusions about overcoming her nursing lot in life. She was brilliant at what she did, and horrible at what she didn't do.

Poor Jacob Renner had never guessed that, though.

Solaina sighed, and leaned restlessly back in her chair, debating whether to go outside to the veranda in order to pass the next hour with some fresh ocean air and morning light, since it was nearly dawn now, and she did so love watching the start of the new day blossom over the beach. Or simply wait here at David's bedside until the next time he roused, or she had to rouse him.

This was her favorite time of the day, really. A cabana chair, a cup of hot tea, and the full splendor of the morning stretching out right before her eyes. Pure heaven, and it was another thing she would miss once she left here. Dharavaj mornings were the most spectacular she had ever seen anywhere, and she couldn't imagine she would find anything to compare to them.

Absently, Solaina pushed herself out of her chair and wandered to the pantry, then opened its mahogany door. She kept little food at the cottage since her time there was so limited and it was easier to take what she needed each time she visited. But there was always a nice array of tea. "Good morning, Earl Grey," she said. No need to break her morning routine because of David. She glanced over at him, wondering if he would be a tea or coffee man. Coming from Toronto, if that was, indeed, where he hailed from and not a figment of his delusions, he could go either way on his beverage choice. Admittedly, she had a taste for caramel macchiato herself. But to start her day that way? "Glad to see you, Earl," she whispered to the tea tin as she drew it out of the pantry. Any port of familiarity in this storm was welcome.

As she poured water into the kettle and set it atop the stove, she watched David thrashing about in the bed. He *was* nice to watch. "So, tea or coffee for you?" she asked, wishing he would wake up for a rational chat on anything, including his morning drink preference. "Or a soda?"

Of course, if he woke up at this very moment, professing his undying love of soda in the morning, what next? He really wasn't so much of a bother, other than the fact that he took up her bed, when she really wanted to be there herself. Alone! And he *was* holding his own against the injuries after all, so all she had to do was keep watch over him until Howard arrived. "Why couldn't you have thrown yourself at another car?" she muttered, striking a match to light the tiny two-burner stove.

Once the water was simmering away, Solaina went to the bed to do another check. Pulse strong, breathing good. "Do you like tea?" she asked, nudging his shoulder to wake him up, just as she'd done every hour. "Because I'm making tea right now, if you'd like some." No coffee, no soda, no choices.

It was her way or none for this interloper, now that she was certain he wasn't going to die on her.

"How did I get here?" he mumbled, looking up at her.

"One step at a time, with me supporting you." That's what she'd told him the last time she'd woken him up and he'd asked. And one other time, a few hours ago.

"Don't remember," he muttered. "Don't remember a damned thing."

"That's because I think you have a concussion." She'd told him that, too, and he'd concurred on a mild one—in a lucid moment, of course. "Which is why I've been waking you up every hour. Don't want you slipping too far in." Old medical protocol, she knew. A good bonk on the head meant waking them up every hour lest they slipped too deep into that concussion and became totally unconscious, or even comatose. Nowadays, sleep wasn't considered such an enemy of a mild head-banger like David's, but she felt better doing it anyway. If nothing else, it gave her something to occupy her time since she couldn't sleep in one-hour bursts like he was doing.

And tonight her sleeplessness had nothing to do with the haunts of Jacob Renner still tilting about in her mind, and everything to do with brand-new images of David Gentry edging out everything but him.

"You need the bed," David mumbled, patting the spot on the mattress next to him.

She laughed. "You're right about that. I do need the bed. Desperately. But my answer is still no. You're in too bad of a shape for all that nonsense, Casanova."

"For all what nonsense?" he asked, his words a bit thick.

"If you can't remember, I'm not going to tell you." She'd given him some ibuprofen on Howard's instructions a couple of hours ago, and now his fever was down a little. She brushed his forehead with the back of her hand to make sure. Ibuprofen and cleaning his wound, plus the fluids he'd taken in his more manageable moments, and he was actually doing much better. It wasn't a fabulous improvement by any means, but enough that she was pleased with his progress. Best of all, she no longer feared, with every breath he drew, that he wouldn't hang on until Howard turned up.

"Was it good?" he asked. "What I offered you?"

"Apparently not, since you don't remember." It had only been a kiss, and truthfully she thought it had been rather charming of him, since a man in his dotty condition might have been begging for so much more. But a chaste kiss suggested to her that David was a gentleman of sorts, and she liked that. "Go back to sleep, David. Maybe next time you wake up you'll remember."

"And will your answer be yes then? Because I'm assuming that up until now it's been no."

She laughed. "In your dreams, Casanova. *In your dreams.*"

"In my dreams, Solaina…"

"How did you know my name?" she asked, as she pulled the bed sheet back up over his shoulders, then adjusted the pillow under his head. She hadn't told him, had she?

"I've always known your name. The lovely Solaina. My pretty lady. How could it be anything else?"

Poor man's having delusions again, Solaina thought as she watched him drift back to sleep. Or maybe she'd mentioned her name to him earlier, and all this lack of sleep was making her as wonky as he was.

Although she still couldn't recall that she had.

"Try taking just a few sips, then I promise I'll leave you

alone for a while." A few sips of tea, a couple of bites of a muffin, an antibiotic, then she'd leave him alone and let him get back to sleep.

He'd been tossing and turning this past hour, and so grumpy throughout this little span of alertness she was just about at her wit's end to know what to do for him…to him…about him… Whoever had said that doctors were the worst patients must have been well acquainted with David Gentry. "So are you lucid, David? Do you understand how badly you need to get this tea in you? Or would you rather have water?" Water or tea. Her only options.

"Don't like Earl Grey," he snapped.

"Did it ever occur to you to tell me that instead of fighting me?"

"Apparently not." He tried to force a smile, then squeezed his eyes shut. "Headache. Can't think straight."

"Concussion. Dehydration. Infection. Take your pick. They'll all give you a headache."

"Am I giving you a headache, pretty lady?"

He was much nicer now, she thought. Mellow and charming again. Casanova. The way she liked him. "A great big one. For the last several hours now." Although it seemed more like several days.

"Don't mean to be so difficult," he said. "But you know what they say about doctors…"

"That they make the kindest, sweetest, most co-operative patients ever known to the medical world. That they drink their fluids and eat their food and take their medicine without a word of protest. And they even volunteer to change their own bed sheets when the time comes. That is what you were going to say, isn't it?"

He chuckled. "And I thought I was the delusional one here."

"Can't blame a girl for trying, can you?" She hurried over to the faucet for a glass of water, then returned to the bed.

"So, where are you from, Solaina?" he asked, taking hold of the water glass, then studying it rather than drinking it. "I detect the slightest hint of French in your voice, but I do hear American there, too."

"I'm from all over. Born in Haiti, raised in Kijé and France. Stayed in the United States for all of my higher education and several years after that for my first job. Then I went to Paris to work and Switzerland for a year, and I worked in Tokyo after that. Now I'm in Dharavaj. At the hospital in Chandella." And in a short while she hoped to be adding a new destination—one yet to be determined—to that travelog. The job offers were coming in, but she hadn't decided which to take. She hadn't yet flipped that proverbial coin. "And you, David? Out there on the road you were asking me to take you home."

"Born, raised and educated in Toronto, and when the time comes I'll be happy to return. But after Toronto I didn't get around quite so much as you. It was Cambodia and…" He sighed deeply and tried to raise the glass to his lips, but his hand was wobbly and a little of the water sloshed over the top and onto the sheet. "So, is this where I get to show you what a good patient I am and change the bed sheet?"

"This is where you get to show me what a good patient you are and drink your water, then eat a bite or two of your muffin. After that, for your dessert, I've got another dose of amoxicillin for you. You're not allergic to it, are you? In one of your coherent moments you told me you weren't." She'd found part of a prescription of it in her medicine cabinet and Howard had instructed her to start him on it immediately.

"No allergies," he said, "and amoxicillin is a broad-spectrum antibiotic, so it should work. Good choice."

"Lucky coincidence. I had some capsules left over from a little lung infection a year ago."

"Didn't your doctor tell you to take all your medicine?" he asked, handing the glass back to her without drinking the water.

"Good thing for you I don't always listen to my doctor." She broke off a small piece of oatmeal muffin and handed it to him.

He took it, ate it, refused a second piece, then shut his eyes. "I'd think I'd like to sleep now."

"And I'd rather be outside, lying on my little stretch of beach, but I can't. Not until you take your pill." She smiled at him. Now that he was cleaned up she could almost envision him as healthy. He was robust, and she wondered how he kept himself in shape. Cycling? Running? Nobody got in the shape David Gentry was in without working at it, and she suspected his great shape was the reason he'd survived his ordeal. Whatever that had been.

"Why don't you let me sleep for another hour, then I'll see what I can do for you…?" David drew in a deep breath, then let it out slowly, fighting to drift off. But not this time. Not until she'd got that antibiotic down him. Playing nice nurse wasn't working, and now it was time to change her game plan. "Oh, no, you don't," she said, shaking him awake. "You can go back to sleep *after* you've done what I've asked. *Not before.* Another sip of water, another bite of muffin, a pill, then you can sleep. Not negotiable, David." She wasn't sounding like a sugar-coated angel of mercy here, and that rather pleased her. Especially when the look on David's face suggested that she was getting through.

"Fine," he snapped. "Whatever you want!"

Grumpy again. Well, so be it. "What I want is for you to take a drink." Instead of letting his hands take hold of the glass, Solaina moved the glass to his lips and held it there as he drank. It was an effort for him, and after mere seconds he was exhausted. Dropping his head back to his pillow, he shut his eyes and fought to control his breathing.

"Out of shape," he whispered.

"I think that if you were out of shape you wouldn't have survived this long," she replied, setting the glass aside and picking up the muffin. "So, are you ready for another bite or two?"

"You don't give up on a man, do you?"

"When a man sleeps in my bed, I get to do whatever I wish. And you, Doctor, are sleeping in my bed, in case you haven't noticed."

"Jasmine. The sheets smell of jasmine. I did notice."

"Not another botanical dissertation," she said, breaking off another bite for him. "You have a flora fixation, David. Did you know that?"

"Right now, I don't know much of anything other than the fact that the most beautiful woman I've ever seen is sitting on the side of the bed, popping muffin bits into my mouth, which should be a very erotic experience, and I'm too damned tired to even chew. Believe me, in my dreams that's not what you were doing. And I was doing a hell of a lot more than fighting my way through a bite of muffin."

"Two bites. You'll be fighting your way through two bites. And, my, aren't you a ruttish one? Even in your condition…"

"I'd have to be dead not to notice you." He reached over and took the muffin from her.

"Three bites, and if you argue that goes up to four. And the last time I tried to feed you I believe the term you used for me was a fat old kouprey."

"And you intend to hold that lapse into insanity against me?"

"Three bites and I won't hold it against you." She smiled at him. "Four bites and it's entirely forgotten."

"There never was a mention of a kouprey, was there?" he asked, before he succumbed to the muffin. "Even in my delirium I would know better than to say something like that about you."

"Four bites," Solaina countered, handing him the first.

"You win," he said, taking it. However, he was able to manage only two bites before fatigue overcame him. "Thank you," he said quietly, as he took the antibiotic pill from her. "And in case I haven't said it…and I really don't remember all I've said, except the kouprey part which I *never* said…thank you for stopping out there on the road and rescuing me. That was brave of you." He raised up, popped the pill into his mouth and washed it down with another drink of water, then collapsed back onto the bed and shut his eyes. "Got to go to sleep now, pretty lady. And dream about…"

Solaina bent over him to feel his forehead. Still feverish, but a little better, owing to the second good cleaning she'd done to his wound and the additional fluids he was getting in him. Soon the antibiotic would kick in fully but, still, David needed so much more than this patch-up job she was doing for him. Surgery to remove the bullet, for starters. Painkillers. X-rays. And here she was equipped with a drink of water, a muffin and a pill. Not enough. She was getting frantic for Howard.

It was daylight now, and warm outside. Not too warm yet, although the hot, moist air would stir later on and chase all but the hearty back inside to sit underneath their overhead fans or in front of their air-conditioning vents.

Solaina liked this time of the day, though. Looked forward to it, actually. Her morning necessities—a pot of tea, a nice muffin, a good book. She glanced through the glass door at the book sitting on the table next to the cabana chair. Another by Marion Lennox—medicine, intrigue, romance all rolled into one. Solaina chuckled. Almost her own life at the moment, minus the part about romance. He *had* called her a fat old kouprey after all. In truth. And that didn't inspire many thoughts of romance.

Besides, she didn't do romance now…didn't get involved. There was no reason to since she didn't commit to staying any place or with anyone for more than the blink of an eye. She was there, then she was gone. No friends, no messy entanglements to untangle. It wasn't the life of her dreams, but it *was* the life of her choosing, and it worked out well enough. Not brilliantly. But adequately, which was all she expected.

Solaina glanced at the Lennox book again and knew that somewhere within those pages, someone would end up entangled, and happy about it. A brilliant ending, a brilliant life. So much better than her own little slice of adequate.

"I'll read it later," she murmured, sighing, as she carried her own tea and muffin outside to her cabana chair and sat down to contemplate the sand and surf. And David—who was fast turning into both a contemplation and an entanglement. "So, what do I do about David?" she asked herself, settling back into her red and yellow canvas sling and shutting her eyes.

The only answer came in the form of the fresh images of him fighting for his life along the side of a dark, deserted highway. Had the timing of the matter been off one way or an-other—her meeting in Chandella ending on time, or her meet-ing going even longer, or her choosing to go back to her little flat instead of heading for her cottage, which was what she'd almost done... There were so many variables in all this, and any one of them coming off differently would have meant that instead of lying in her bed, causing her huge problems in lo-gistics, proximity and, worst of all, medical capability, David Gentry might be...

No, he *would* be dead. She may not be the queen of clini-cal practice when it came to performing any nursing skills, but it didn't take much in the way of actual patient skill to make that diagnosis. David would have died of exposure some time last night.

Hard to imagine, considering his strong rally this morning. Still, Solaina shivered, thinking about it. David dead. No! That wasn't an image she wanted emblazoned alongside Jacob Renner's. All too much to see in her dreams, so she opened her eyes and focused on the white sands stretching out in front of her. Any more fixation on David right now would force her to weigh her decisions concerning him. He was sta-ble. He wasn't going to die in her bed. He wasn't bleeding. He didn't even seem to be in too much pain.

Good enough for now. And soon Howard would be here to take charge. All she had to do was wait, which seemed infinitely harder to her than those Christmas mornings when she had been a child and her parents had insisted on a proper family breakfast before she and Solange had been allowed to rip into all those gifts under the tree. She'd never thought there could have been a wait as long as that. Until now.

Impatiently, Solaina picked up the Lennox book and turned to the first page. She really had hated those family breakfasts on Christmas morning! And this!

CHAPTER FOUR

DAVID stirred around in bed, then finally found a relatively comfortable position flat on his back, staring up at the ceiling. This time when he woke up he knew exactly where he was and why he was there. Last time it had taken him a few minutes, and somewhere in his distant recollections he seemed to recall a petulant little schoolboy being quite cranky with his nurse. "Could have been a dream." he muttered. The half-eaten muffin and the half-filled glass of water sitting on the table next to the bed told him otherwise.

He wanted to call out for her. *Solaina.* Beautiful name. Beautiful woman. He'd thought so the first time he'd ever seen her. When had it been? He couldn't quite remember. Had it been last night when she'd rescued him on the road? Or a month ago in Chandella? Six months ago in Switzerland? Right now those memories were smudged. They were there, but buried deep and not making too much sense to him. But they would. Memories that came with Solaina were meant to be the memories that lasted a lifetime.

His memories of what had happened in Cambodia were smudged over, too. He recalled getting the call. It had been a routine ambulance run, as routine as any run to pick up a landmine victim would be. He'd done that many times from his little hospital outside Kantha, gone to rescue someone who'd tripped over a mine planted three decades ago.

But right now he didn't recall the particulars of this run—the one that had landed him in the bed of the woman whose bed he'd most wanted to land in. Considering his condition, though, something had gone horribly wrong, and he couldn't remember what. Meaning he could still be in trouble, which wasn't acceptable at all because he might be involving the beautiful Solaina in his mess as well.

"So you get the hell out of here before what you've done comes down on her," he said aloud, thinking over, essentially, the only option he had. He wasn't going to die. Not now. Even in his wooly headed condition he knew that much. So maybe he could go somewhere else, figuratively lick his wounds until he was well enough to get back to Kantha. And then what? Hope she didn't get messed up in his fallout?

David pulled back the sheets and raised himself up to look at his body. Having his ribs kicked and broken was coming back to him. The black, steel-toed boot. The warnings to get out of Cambodia, get out of Dharavaj. He remembered all that now. The man who'd dragged him from the Hummer—at first David had thought it was a highway robber out to take his vehicle. But then he'd called him by name. "Are you Dr Gentry?" the man had screamed at him.

At gunpoint. He remembered that, too. The barrel of that gun pointed at him. But it had been such a preposterously small gun he'd never expected the man to use it. Just a tiny, pearl-handled spot of a thing in the palm of his hand. A honker of an AK-47 would have made more sense.

Or maybe he was fuzzy again. His head did hurt like hell.

And his hands were still shaking like a Chihuahua having a nervous breakdown.

Well, one thing was for sure, *fuzzy or not,* someone had done a nasty job on him. Tried to kick him to death, judging from the look of things. At least, that's what he would diagnose if this had happened to one of his patients.

He ran his hands down his ribs and sucked in a sharp breath as the pain kicked in. Sharp. Deep. It was cutting right straight through him, and he was glad of every agonizing sensation, because it sure beat the alternative. Which was, just hours ago, looking to be a rather eternal bout with the quietus. In spite of pain, though, Solaina had certainly done a good job of dressing his wounds. She had a nice touch…the lovely Solaina. A nice touch he desperately wanted to remember the next time he woke up. Of course, he'd thought he'd remembered her the last time he'd woken up, and perhaps the time before that. But he wasn't sure… Wasn't sure about anything except that someone like Solaina…and her touch…needed to be remembered.

Gingerly, David flexed his shoulder, probing gently over the bandage with his fingertips. He'd removed enough bullets in his time to know this one was only in the flesh. At least for starters, because by now he was sure the infection from something that had commenced as barely a scratch was raging deep. Raging, spreading… It should have killed him, and probably would have. Mercifully, Solaina again.

Sitting up a little more, David saw her standing in the doorway, watching him.

"Going somewhere?" she asked.

Backlit against the sun streaming in, she was in silhouette, leaving her exact detail to his imagination. Even in his bleariness, he'd memorized that detail, memorized it from that very first instant. "Do I know you?" he asked. "Have we met before?"

"Is that a come-on, Casanova? Because, if it is, it's not very original."

"Not a come-on. At least, I don't think it is." He smiled at her. "But if it was, did it work?"

She laughed. "Silly me, thinking that everything you said when you were delusional was delusional."

"And you have me at a disadvantage, since I don't recall what I said. But I do recall you. So, you and me. We haven't…"

She gave her head a vehement shake. "We haven't."

"Pity," he said, lying back down. He was too weak, he had no idea where he was…all good reasons to sleep for a while longer before he did anything so drastic as to walk, or crawl, as the case might be, out of there. "Because I thought that for once in my life I was showing some extraordinarily good taste."

"That flattery will get you another antibiotic, Doctor." She crossed over to the bed and felt his forehead. "I think your fever's coming down quite nicely now."

"Good nursing care will do it every time."

She spun away from him and headed to the tiny kitchen area. "Don't ever confuse what I'm doing for you as good nursing care, Doctor. That could be a fatal error in judgement."

"But you are a nurse. Correct? I wasn't dreaming that, was I?"

"I have a nursing certificate, yes," she said.

Her demeanor switched from warm to icy cold so quickly, David wondered if she'd told him something else he was forgetting.

"But having my certificate doesn't make me a nurse. At least, not in the abilities you've come to expect from a nurse. I direct a nursing program, make administrative decisions, prepare budgets, have meetings with the board of directors. And I never go near patients."

"The bandages are good," he said, running his hand over his chest. "Expert job of getting me strapped up."

"*Anybody* can apply a bandage." She took a deep breath to steady herself. "Now, would you care for something to eat? Fruit salad, maybe? Or I could cook some rice."

He shook his head. Truth was, he wanted to know more about her. What made her so edgy on the subject of nursing? And why did someone so glorious coop herself up in this tiny hole? The mental part of him wanted it anyway. The physical part of him wanted sleep again. Two minutes awake and he could already feel his bedraggled body dragging him right back down. "So did I tell you I'm a surgeon?" he asked, more to keep himself alert than for the purpose of meaningful conversation. He liked talking to Solaina. Liked listening to her. Liked watching her when they weren't talking.

"You told me your name. I knew you were a surgeon. By reputation."

He wasn't sure how far he should go with this. Finding a way out of here was probably the better choice next time he came around. Someplace far, far away from her. Someplace so that her not being around him would guarantee her safety. But damn! Even trying to raise his head off the bed was more effort than he was capable of. "Tell me about my reputation. That seems to be one of the things I'm blurry over. And maybe just a couple of small bites of fruit would be nice. My stomach seems to be in a bit of a roil."

Solaina pulled a star fruit from a basket sitting on the counter next to the tiny kitchen sink and ran it under the running water. Then she pulled a paring knife from the drawer and began peeling. "I'd heard you were a very good surgeon. By reputation, maybe one of the best in the area."

"And?"

Solaina sliced the star fruit into a bowl and pulled out a white, pulpy mangosteen and broke it open, dropping the sections into the same bowl. Her third selection was a Japanese pear that resembled a yellow apple more than a pear. "And that's it. Except *jai ron*. Do you know *jai ron*?" Hot heart.

"You think I have *jai ron*?" He chuckled.

"Even in your delusions, Casanova."

David watched Solaina pull a durian from the fruit basket then return it. The durian was the most expensive of all Dharavaj fruit, and probably the oddest. A delicacy actually, it was not too bad to the taste when combined with coconut milk or sticky rice. But it had a horribly repugnant smell, and personally he'd never developed a fondness for it. The locals loved it, though. They revered it, in fact, and for the *farang*—foreigners—who weren't brave enough to venture past its smell, there was always durian ice cream, durian cake and even durian chewing gum. But he'd never braved those forms of the fruit either.

Funny how he remembered all that. And, yes, he did seem to recall some blather about a rhododendron. "I didn't guess you for a durian. You seem more the pineapple or coconut or strawberry type."

"You never know, do you?" she asked, wrinkling her nose at him. "Although I will say a strawberry is much better than a durian."

Suddenly, David caught himself fantasizing about Solaina eating a strawberry…her luscious lips on that succulent, red fruit… *"Jai ron,"* he murmured. Solaina was a woman who would make any man's heart blaze; even a man in his precarious condition. "And I suppose you would be *jai yen?*" Cool heart, or calm.

Solaina smiled as she carried the bowl of fruit over to the bed. "Not *jai yen* so much as *krienjai.*" One who avoided confrontation. "That is, until I met you last night, and since then you've been one big confrontation for me, Doctor."

"For which I apologize."

"Accepted." She sat the bowl of fruit on the table next to the bed. "So, in order to maintain my status as *krienjai*, I need to figure out what to do with you. Any suggestions? Perhaps after my friend has had a look at you I can take you to Chandella. It's a long drive, but that's where I live and I'm used to it."

Chandella? He needed Kantha. He wanted to alert the minister of police about this latest attack, then get back to normalcy. Or try and get back to normalcy and hope that whatever this vendetta was, it was over. And pray that he hadn't involved Solaina in any way. "A little more rest and I'll be able to leave on my own." He wasn't sure how far he would get, but if someone was after him, she would be safer without him.

Solaina chuckled. "The people of Dharavaj may be liberal-minded, but I don't imagine the sight of you wandering down the road in your condition, without your pants, is going to go unnoticed. I think you'd better have another think on that before you set out."

His pants. He hadn't thought about that. If he remembered correctly, she'd cut them up last night and bandaged him with the strips. So no pants seemed the end of that round, since right then he didn't have enough reserves to try for another plan of escape—one without his pants. Rather, he invested in a piece of the star fruit, then a bite of the Japanese pear. Then he lay back and shut his eyes, resigning himself to whatever lot his fair captor had in mind for the next little while. "Since I can't leave without my pants, when I wake up again, I think you need to do a little surgery on me," he said as he drifted away.

"I'll cut your fruit, David. But that's all I'll cut. Remember *krienjai*?"

Settling down into her cabana chair with a nice *naam phon-la-mai*—the fruit juice she had blended from the fruit David hadn't eaten—Solaina picked up her Marion Lennox book and opened it to the second chapter. Even without David in her bed, this was how she would have spent the weekend. Reading, relaxing, dozing… So, no reason to do otherwise just because her bed was in other ways occupied.

Solaina sighed contentedly, settling in. She was almost through the first paragraph when a crash that nearly shook the thin cottage walls, followed by a string of profanity, ripped right through the closed veranda doors.

Solaina dropped the book on the bamboo floor and jumped up from her sling chair, then flew back inside, only to find David on the floor next to the overturned bedside table, his shoulder bleeding. Sitting there among the shards of the broken water glass and her little Buddha, he looked more angry than injured, and Solaina thought it best not to ask him what had happened. She knew. Another little bout with delirium most likely, and he was getting up—probably to leave.

Slipping into some leather-soled huaraches, she walked over to where David was pulling himself out of the wreckage. "You've opened your shoulder wound," she said, holding out a hand to help him stand. There was no other obvious injury. Except to his ego, probably. And that was a wound she wouldn't even pretend to touch.

"Bullet's gotta come out this time," he grumbled, righting himself, then falling back into the bed. "Risking infection to the bone. I was coming to get you."

"Which means?" She had a hunch—change that to a sick feeling in the pit of her stomach—that the next words out of his mouth were going to be something like, *You can do it, Solaina.* Which, of course, she could not.

"Which means a simple procedure. You cut, I bite the bullet. Five-minute procedure. That's all."

His eyes fluttered shut and Solaina nudged him. "I can't do it, David!" Can't, wouldn't. She had no equipment, no skills. Panic started rising and immediately Jacob Renner sprang to mind, as he always did. Then her hands started trembling, as they always did. But she reined in the breathing and fought off the lightheadedness before they overcame her. *Deep breath…slowly. Focus, Laina. Focus.*

Jacob Renner—that incident always came back when she thought she could do something. But she'd learned the awful truth at the cost of poor Jacob's life. *She could not.* "Look, David," she said, fighting to maintain her carriage, "the biggest delusion you've had so far is that I can do this for you. But I cannot. I don't have the skills. You're just going to have to wait until my friend gets here." She glanced at the clock on the kitchenette wall. Twelve hours since she'd called him. The roads in Dharavaj were often indirect, and not in good shape. But surely he wouldn't be much longer.

"OK, if not you, Solaina. Me. I can do this."

"You?" Solaina sputtered. "You're not delusional, David. You're crazy!" She saw him glancing over toward the kitchenette. "Now, if you'll excuse me for a moment, I think I'll just go hide all the knives. And in case you don't remember me saying this a dozen times, I have a friend *en route* to take care of you."

Howard Brumley, a British transplant to Chandella, and Solaina's neighbor, was a very good surgeon. He'd retired to travel the world with his wife, Victoria, and had made it no further than Dharavaj, the Brumleys' first and only stop on their worldwide jaunt. Now they were like family to her, even though, admittedly, she didn't see them nearly often enough. Howard and Victoria were both godsends to her right now, and she trusted them like she trusted no one else except her sister.

"I'm not waiting for your friend," David replied, his voice too calm for the situation. He was lucid, and determined. A dangerous combination in his condition. The man was either crazy in the truest sense of the word, and having nothing to do with his present condition, or he was the bravest man she'd ever met. And at the moment she wasn't leaning one way or another on which he was.

"He has a scalpel, David. A real scalpel and not a kitchen knife. And antiseptic and forceps. He's a qualified surgeon, and he has everything he needs to do it the right way." A surgeon with advanced arthritis in his hands, which had been a worry to her since he'd retired. "For a weak man—and one who doesn't have a pair of pants, in case you've forgotten— you're being awfully argumentative about this."

"Not argumentative. Practical."

"Weak," she countered. "Weak, strong-willed, very opinionated. And none of that leads to being practical, when you're threatening to take out your bullet with one of my kitchen knives." Briefly, Solaina wondered how strong he might be when he recovered. She had always had a fascination with strong men. Strong physically was nice, of course, but that's not what she meant. She was thinking strong in the ways that counted—morals and principles. "And he's bringing you some pants, too," she continued. "Which is very practical for a man in your condition. So, no options, David. No kitchen knives either. We wait. Or you can get up and walk right out of here and take your chances." Of course, she knew that he knew he couldn't.

"I'm sorry about everything I've put you through," David said. "About breaking the glass, and your lamp. And that little Buddha. About being so grumpy, too."

Solaina glanced at the little porcelain bedside lamp, which was now a mound of fragments lying in the bottom of the waste basket. And, wistfully, her Buddha. It was only a trinket, she knew. But losing him made her a little sad. Funny, now that it was gone, she recalled how often she'd looked at it just to make herself smile. "Technically, it's not my lamp since I only rent the cottage," she said. "But apology accepted for the lamp. And for being grumpy, too. After what you've been through, I suppose you deserve to be grumpy. But can I ask you one thing?" His head propped up on a stack of pillows and with his hands behind his head, the sheet covering him to the waist, David was the picture of casual charm all sprawled in the middle of the bed. He was putting on a brave grin, but she could see the worry behind it, the concern in his eyes that even his forced twinkle couldn't cover.

"With what I've put you through, you're entitled to ask me anything you want."

"But does that mean you'll answer anything I ask?"

"For you, pretty lady, anything."

Solaina laughed. "I don't know whether to believe that or not."

"I've done a lot of things in my life, been a lot of things, said a lot of things. But here's something you can count on. I'll never lie to you. You may not like the truth you'll hear from me, but it will always be the truth."

"Another line?"

"I suppose that's for you to decide, isn't it?" He shifted position gingerly, sliding down a little further into the bed. "So are you always this wary of everyone, or is it just me bringing out the wariness in you?"

"Just you," she said, trying to sound neutral. The truth was, she wasn't nearly as wary of David as he might have guessed. She was wary of his expectations of her, and maybe a few little niggling feelings popping up for him, but not *of* him.

"And that, pretty lady, was a lie. You don't do it well, you know. Those beautiful eyes tell me everything. Although I will say, you're perfectly justified in being wary of me. You're not the first who has been, and you certainly won't be the last."

"So why are people wary of you, David?"

"Is that the question you wanted to ask me? Because I think I'm going down for another nap in just a second or two."

"One of the questions," she replied, walking over to the kitchen. He needed another antibiotic, only this time she would give him the remainder of her *naam phon-la-mai,* except *she* would hold the glass since there were but three left in the cottage. "I have more, but I think that's a good place to start."

"And just when I thought you were about to enquire about my marital status."

"I would if I were interested," she said, removing the pitcher from the tiny refrigerator. "But I'm not, so I'll stick to my original question. Why are people wary of you?"

"No, I'm not."

She glanced over at him in time to see him mask a smile. It was nice having someone here for a change, she decided. Someone smiling at her from her bed. How long had it been since that had happened, for whatever reason?

"You're not what, David?" she asked, even though she knew exactly what he was answering.

"I'm not married, engaged, trapped, committed, or casually involved."

Solaina shook her head skeptically. "Not according to the papers in your wallet," she teased. "I saw the picture of your wife and three children. Nice-looking family. And you have a cocker spaniel, David. Cute little dog. Cute kids, too. What were their names again? You kept mumbling them when you were delirious, but I've forgotten them already."

"I'm not that loopy." He laughed, glancing at his ring finger for a quick check.

"But I had you thinking that you might be, didn't I?" This was a delicious little bit of banter between them. Delicious and natural. For a moment she almost fancied it into her future, but she pulled back on that thought before it got too far. This was a delicious little bit of banter between them, and that's all that it was.

"OK, I'll answer your question before you convince me that I'm a totally certifiable lunatic. Or I convince myself of it." He chuckled. "People are wary of me because I'm blunt. I don't have a lot of time to waste, or finesse if I think you're wasting my time, and I tend to be a little more forward and exacting than I probably should be. Or a lot more, actually. Plus, I'm stubborn, I don't always follow the rules—"

"That's more than I wanted to know," Solaina said, holding up her hand to stop him as she sat down on the edge of the bed. "So how about you just take this pill, and I'll imagine the rest?" Howard had instructed her to bump up his dosage. Double it, triple it if she could. From what she could see in David's response, it was working. He was much better.

"Told you I'm honest."

"So you're what? Thirty-five?"

"Thirty-six."

"OK. You're thirty-six, your wallet doesn't have pictures of the wife and kiddies. No cocker spaniel either. And according to IMO, you went home a while ago. So why would they be saying something like that when you're obviously not back in Toronto?"

"Because they don't know, I suppose." He sucked in a deep breath. "They were downsizing their unit in Cambodia. I wanted to stay, they wanted me to go. So I did, only not with them, and I suppose that once I was out the door, they simply didn't follow me."

"What did you do that got you into this shape?"

"Wrong place, wrong time, I suppose."

"And that's it?"

He shrugged. "People get mugged worldwide."

"And there's no cause for alarm. Is that what you're telling me?" Solaina offered him a second sip of the fruit juice. He pushed her hand away, so she drank it instead. "I think you're the master of the understatement, David. Or evasion. I don't know which."

"Right now, the only thing I'm the master of is an aching rib cage and a sore shoulder. And, believe me, there's no evasion in that." He slid down into the bed and pulled the sheet entirely over his chest. "Maybe I will just take that nap now and wait until your friend arrives." Then he shut his eyes.

"And the doctor falls asleep just in the nick of time," Solaina murmured, bending down until her lips grazed his ear. "Or else you would have had to tell me the *real* truth behind David Gentry," she whispered. "The one where you reveal why someone would do this to you."

Turning away, Solaina went back outside to the veranda, and her book.

He'd watched her read for almost an hour now. *Mesmerized.* That was the perfect word to describe the way he was feeling. Watching Solaina mesmerized him. Her every movement was so deliberate, yet so graceful—the way she turned a page, the way she picked up her drink, the way she tilted the brim of the straw hat she was wearing to keep the sun out of her eyes. She was something to watch, and he was more than glad to surrender yet another round of sleep to do just that.

Now that his mind was functioning better, he recalled the first time he'd seen Solaina. It had been, what? Just over a month ago, at the hospital in Chandella, he thought. He had been rather scruffy that day, just in from the jungle to check on a patient. Baggy khaki cargo shorts, a week's growth of beard, a T-shirt with a ripped sleeve, wild hair that hadn't seen a comb in a while. She would have looked right past him had he been in a place where she might have seen him. But he hadn't been. His visits to the city were always a low-key affair, so not to attract too much attention.

Certainly, the Dharavaj government knew about his little hospital. He wasn't operating under the radar in that respect, and he was licensed after all. The government was also generous enough to help secure visas for those who came over the border for medical treatment without the legalities in place. A few dollars and a couple of days, and the paperwork was in order.

But, still, the very nature of his hospital caused speculation because he wasn't doing business in the traditional sense most people expected of hospitals. And it went against the grain of IMO, which always stayed above the radar in its operations. Which was the core of his problem. There were so many people under that radar who needed help—the ones without real identities, the ones without homes, the ones without a country. IMO was benevolent, but it required those things from its patients: names to put on the wristband; a city of residence; a nationality.

Over in Cambodia, IMO took care of the people who could provide those things. In Dharavaj, David took care of the ones who could not. And IMO had disowned him for it. His departure had been a slap at their system. And him going into their territory to bring back patients to his hospital was an insult. But one with which he could live.

Six months away from IMO and out on his own, he was pleased with the progress he was making. His surgery was set up well, his physical therapy department was established. So, even if his hospital was not an overt endeavor in the truest sense of the word, it was a good one, and the one for which he'd searched for the entirety of his career. Maybe even before that.

Getting to the heart of the need—that's all he'd ever wanted. And now he had it.

As he drifted off, David closed his eyes to conjure up the memory of the first time he'd seen Solaina. She had been in a two-piece, orchid-colored suit, hair up, just a touch of make-up…she smelt of jasmine that day, too. She'd rushed right past him, leading her group of nurses, and he'd smelled the jasmine and been fixated on it ever since.

Women had come and gone in his life. Just ask his wife. In one door and out the other without much notice. Permanent relationships just stifled. Or had the life sucked out of them. But Solaina was the memory that lingered on, the dream he begged for at night, the spontaneous smile that happened to him when he most needed to smile. Then to meet her the way he had…to literally run into her car. He chuckled. "Meant to be, Davey," he murmured. "That's the only way to describe it. You meeting Solaina like that was meant to be."

Even though he said the words, he wasn't so sure he believed them. Meeting her had been on his mind all these weeks now, and he could have—any day, any time. He'd known who she was, where she was. And even though he'd returned to the hospital twice after that first time he'd seen her, he'd purposely stayed away from the places he might stumble into her. Why? "Coward," he muttered, although it was much more than that. What a woman like Solaina could do to a man like him *really* scared him, and that was the crux of his cowardice.

He really did want to find out what a woman like Solaina could do to him, which meant calamity. His first-time disaster had cost him six years. Five in the marriage and one on the skids, trying to get over it. Court battles, personal battles, infidelity…failed medical practice afterwards, woman after woman. He'd crawled back out of the dark days scarred and limping, figuratively, and had found his place. And it had had nothing to do with all the extraneous trappings. A kindly man with impeccable medical credentials had specialed him, helped him get back on track, then set him on a plane to Cambodia.

Now he was happy, settled, and no way was he willing to take the risk again. Not fair to him, and especially not fair to anyone with whom he was involved…Solaina.

Sighing, David rubbed his hand over his sore ribs and watched her shift in her chair outside, crossing her left leg over her right. The slight movement took his mind off the melancholia overtaking him, and he was glad of the distraction. She was in short shorts now, and her legs… Perfect. Long, slender, dark. Drawing in a breath almost hurt, just thinking about the most beautiful legs he had ever seen.

"Solaina," he whispered. "Why you? Why now?"

CHAPTER FIVE

"WHEN did you get here?" Solaina gasped, dropping her book to the floor. She'd enjoyed it but, just like always, she felt mellow at the end. Happy endings always made her mellow, and today especially she was well past mellow and on her way to melancholia. Not because of the book, but because her life never turned out like the stories in the books she read. And perhaps there was still a bit of the little girl in her with the childish notion that everyone deserved a happy ending. Her own ending, however, was only adequate thus far, which by many standards was better than most. So she didn't complain, even if she did have some leftover longings. "I didn't hear you come up."

Solaina jumped up to greet Howard. He was a portly bear of a man, bushy white hair, bushy white beard. She styled him as a jolly Santa because, apart from his physical attributes, he *was* jolly, with a laugh that never failed to cheer her up. Could she have chosen a father, she would have chosen Howard.

"We came up from the side of the cottage. Victoria didn't want to go inside just yet. She said since this was a house call she was going to make good use of the beach this afternoon and leave all the medical bothers to us. So before we get to the particulars, I've come to fetch her a *naam phon-la-mai,* if you have some made. Nothing with that dreaded durian, however. It has such a stink, no matter what people say. Victoria was quite specific about not wanting it."

"None of that dreaded durian," Solaina said, falling into Howard's open arms. "I'm so glad you're here, Howard."

"How have you been, dear?" he asked. "We haven't seen as much of you lately as we would have liked. And I do apologize for taking so long to get here. Normally, a meandering road is a pleasant one to a man who doesn't drive so quickly any more. But unfortunately it can also become a dreadfully slow curse."

"I'm so sorry I pulled you away from your holiday, Howard. And never you mind about how long it took to get here. I'm just thrilled that you could come at all."

"Since I retired, life is but one long holiday, you know, so don't concern yourself about pulling me away. I'm just glad I can be of some help to you. And just between us, I don't think my bottom would have gone in for another ride on an elephant. Victoria was enjoying our day excursions, but let's just say I was getting a little weary of the lurching of the pachyderm." He chuckled. "Coming here to help my favorite woman in the world, next to Victoria, has saved me a rather unsavory injury, I think." He gave Solaina a fatherly kiss on the forehead. "So where have you been keeping yourself, besides holed up here with your patient?" Howard asked quietly, following Solaina through the veranda doors.

"Busy at the hospital, trying to finish off all my affairs before I leave."

"You're still thinking of leaving, are you?" he asked. "I'd rather thought you'd put that notion out of your head, if for no other reason than Victoria and I cannot do without you."

Solaina laughed. "I'll still be in Dharavaj for a while, until I've decided which post to take. And you know I'll be back to see you as often as I can."

"We don't see you often enough as it is and we live just next door. So you'll forget about us soon enough. You'll send a card at Christmas for a year or two, then scratch us off your list." Howard drew in a long, exaggerated sigh. "Victoria is most upset about this, you know. She's not going to be at all pleasant about you leaving us when the time comes."

Solaina handed the glass of *naam phon-la-mai* to Howard and shooed him out the door to his wife. "You tell Victoria to enjoy the beach, and that as soon as you've had a look at my patient in here, we'll both be out to join her."

"You, my dear, along with my precious wife, may enjoy the sand between your toes, but I'll stay on the veranda and add a little grog to my *naam phon-la-mai*. Perhaps your guest might be well enough by then to join me in a nip. Good for what ails him, you know."

Solaina glanced over at David and wondered if he was sleeping or faking. "Perhaps by then my guest will be gone, and you can have all the grogged *naam phon-la-mai* for yourself."

Howard arched his bushy eyebrows and winked. "Some things are much better shared, my dear. Pity you haven't experienced that in your life yet, but Victoria and I are still holding out some hope for you. You're not a frump after all, and I should think some man would find you suitable." He glanced sideways at David, and a broad smiled crossed his face.

"Suitable? I think it's the other way around, Howard. If I'm in the market, I'll be the one to find the young man suitable." Solaina laughed, glancing over at David, too, just in time to see a big, fat grin cross his face. Before she could open her mouth to say a word, Howard gave her a friendly peck on the cheek and trotted away, *naam phon-la-mai* in hand, to his wife. "So stop your grinning," Solaina said, once Howard was out of earshot.

"He's right, you know. You're not a frump."

"Whether or not I'm a frump is not your concern," she said, spinning around to the veranda door to wave to Victoria, who was wrestling an umbrella pole into the sand.

"Testy, aren't you? Or is that defensive more than testy, because of what your friend said?"

"You know what? I think I'll have a try at that bullet in your shoulder with my fingernails," she said, her back still to him. "After I sharpen them. You really don't need a bullet to bite down on, do you?"

"Believe me, since I've met you, Solaina, I've dreamt about biting down on many things, and a bullet was never, ever one of them."

Solaina turned slowly to face him. "In your dreams, Doctor," she said, a slow, earthy smile spreading over her face.

"Speaking of which…"

When his eyes fluttered shut again, she breathed a sigh of relief. No point in making this personal, although it was becoming obvious that it could be. She had places to go, David had things to do, and neither of them were on the same path.

Too bad, she thought as a heavy-hearted feeling started seeping all the way down to her toes. *Too bad.*

"In my dreams, Solaina," David murmured as he drifted away. "Always in my dreams."

"You have David Gentry?" Howard Brumley chuckled as he rubbed his bearded chin. "That's rather a hotbed of controversy to be lying in just about now, isn't it?" he asked Solaina. "All that situation with him and IMO going round and round, then him walking out on them like he did and starting up on his own. Sticky, indeed. And now here you are, someone who helps train their nurses, stuck right in the middle of it."

"What do you mean, walking out on them? He said he had a disagreement and left, but I didn't get the impression he'd gone out and started up on his own. At least, he didn't mention that." They were outside on the veranda, the door closed, and no matter if David was asleep or awake he couldn't hear this conversation—the one he'd been keeping from her that she wanted to hear. "Tell me what you know, Howard. And, more specifically, do you think someone at IMO might have it out for him so badly they would do this to him?"

"Let me answer the last part of that first. IMO is full of doctors and nurses and, David was generally well respected in IMO. So I can't imagine one of them took a berserk notion to whack him about. Of course, starting up on his own has ruffled more than a few of the top-flight IMO feathers. It's made them re-evaluate their mission and start to tidy up their own little house. Or so I've heard." He chuckled. "Funny how he ended up here, isn't it? And with you starting up that training program to send nurses off to IMO."

"Just two days' orientation to the region. The illnesses, the bugs, the poisonous snakes. That's all we've been doing in Chandella." Her contribution to what she thought was a worthy cause. For another month anyway. Then she'd be gone.

Howard drew in a deep sigh, then let it out slowly. "Your patient is a bit of a rabble-rouser, by the way. As he left IMO, he made a comment about them being a festering boil on somebody's bottom. They didn't take kindly to that, since it made the newspapers."

"But they harbor him no ill will?"

"On the contrary, they harbor him quite a lot of ill will, I should think. But I don't think they'd beat him up over it."

That was one of the things she loved most about Howard. He was almost too civilized for his own good. Always the optimist, always the caring humanitarian.

"Well, someone took a boot and a gun to him, for whatever reason, then he threw himself into the side of my car and I've been dealing with him ever since. And you know how I feel about that."

"I suppose I do! You're the young lady who won't get involved. How very noble of you, sparing some deserving young man your charms."

"Do you mean some deserving young man who doesn't mind dismantling his life and following me whenever I get the whim?"

"I should think that once you know your foible, you could correct it."

"Foible?" Solaina laughed. "The only foible I can see in what I do is becoming involved with a charming man who thinks my lifestyle is only a foible and not a choice."

"Yet you protest it so vehemently. It makes me think that your thoughts are running much closer to mine than you'd care to admit."

"We all can't be as happy as you are, Howard. You are one of the lucky ones who's had everything."

"So you're admitting that your life doesn't make you happy?"

He was a dear man, and she adored him. But he'd been persistent about her happiness for such a long time now that she was worn out on the subject. Her life was what it was, what she made it.

"Well, if it's of any consequence, your David is a brilliant surgeon. And what he's doing out there…"

"Out where?" she interrupted.

"A nice little town called Kantha. And a lovely little hospital he calls Vista. They take care of landmine casualties among the rurals mostly. The farmers, the rice pickers, the people who wander about from place to place, looking for work—and that doesn't include you, dear. Although that's what you do, isn't it?"

He just wasn't going to get off the subject of her. Instead of fussing with him, she decided to keep the conversation focused on David, no matter how much Howard wanted to divert it. "But he hasn't said anything about a hospital."

"He *has* been quite sick, and didn't you say his favorite topic is shrubbery or some sort?"

"When he's out of his head he does like to go on about bushes. But he's had moments when he's not been so daft, and he still didn't say anything." Of course, what he did in the outside world was none of her business. *That's the smartest way to go, Laina. Stay completely uninvolved.* That's what her brain was telling her anyway. But part of her really did want to know more about him. After all, it wasn't every day she got to bring a total stranger into her bed, even if it was only to nurse him until better medical help arrived.

"Well, it is a bit of a clandestine affair after all. Not exactly well hidden, but not exactly out in the open. Discretion is the better part of valor, and all that."

"Yet you know about it."

"I know about a great many things, dear."

"So in your vast vault of personal knowledge, is there anything else about him that you can recall?" she asked.

"That's all there is to say, really. At least, all I know to tell you. Your friend took a couple of their best doctors with him when he left, and that's all I can say on the matter." Howard raised a finger to his lips to shush her before she could ask anything else, then strolled over to David's bedside.

"Dr Gentry, I presume?" He chuckled.

"Only if you come bearing forceps, because I'm ready to get the bullet out of my shoulder any way I have to."

"Long forceps, Doctor. And a nice, sharp scalpel if I'm in need of a good cut to cure my surgical lusts."

"It's nice to see you, Howard," David said. "Pardon me for not shaking hands with you, but my shaking arm is otherwise occupied."

"You two know each other?" Solaina sputtered. "Why didn't you say something to me, Howard?"

"To be honest, I didn't know it was him. Didn't know who it was until I came in to fetch Victoria's *naam phon-la-mai*. I must say, I was a bit surprised, as he's been missing for a while."

"But *you* didn't tell me you knew him when I did mention his name."

"And *you* didn't ask if I did. So we're even." Howard snapped on a pair of rubber gloves he'd brought with him and began to peel away the bandage from David's shoulder. "Nasty little wound," he said, more to himself than to either David or Solaina. "Good bit of infection going on, too. No gangrene that I can see, though."

"Like I said, he's been feverish," Solaina said. "And delusional off and on. He talks to trees and shrubs."

"Talks *about* trees and shrubs," David corrected her, then gritted his teeth for what was about to come. Howard was standing over him, uncapping the bottle of alcohol—and it wasn't the kind meant to be ingested.

"I think this is going to hurt like hell," Howard said. "But I need to get in to do a nice deep clean before I do anything else, and this is the fastest way to do it."

Solaina turned away. Even a little alcohol on a tiny cut brought tears to her eyes, and there was no way she wanted to watch something that painful happening to David.

"No, dear. You don't get to close your eyes for this one," Howard said. "You're a nurse, and I need a nurse."

"You know what kind of nurse I am," Solaina protested.

"A very good one at what you do, and a very good one over-all, I suspect, even though you won't admit it. But you've done a splendid job with David so far, Solaina. Remarkable, in fact. When I first talked to you last night and you described his con-dition, I expected to find someone just a breath or two away from being a memory. His infection is much better since you cleaned his wound earlier and I think the antibiotics are work-ing. You've hydrated him nicely without the benefit of an IV and gotten a little nourishment into him. You've patched up those ribs so they don't burst his lung. A good job of it, indeed.

"In fact, if you'd ever care to come out from behind your desk, I think you'd make a very good practicing nurse. And just to prove my point, what you're going to do right now is be my hands. I'll hold the lad down and you'll yank the bul-let out of his arm." He grinned at her through his beard. "A simple procedure, really. All it takes is two good hands, which I no longer have."

"Me?" she sputtered. "You want me to remove the bullet?"

Solaina shook her head frantically. "No," she choked, stepping back from Howard. "I can't do that. I can't operate on him!"

"And with the arthritis in my hands, you expect me to?" Howard held up his hands to prove his point, and even through the surgical gloves his swollen, bent knuckles were obvious. "So unless you expect David to do the job himself…" He handed a pair of surgical gloves to Solaina, which she tossed aside immediately. "Piece of cake, dear. You probe the wound, then when you find the bullet you grab hold and yank it out."

"And if I don't find the bullet?"

"You try again." He looked down at David, frowning. "I don't have any drugs, but would a spot of whiskey set you up for this?"

"More than a spot," David said. "Maybe two or three."

"A good man knows the value of good liquor. Straight?" he asked.

"Straight. No point in making it a social drink with all the extras, is there, when all I want to do is kill the pain?"

"Howard!" Solaina snapped. "He's been delirious off and on for the better part of the night and day. And you're offering him…"

"An anesthetic. Medicinal purposes only." He laughed heartily. "Unless you'd rather make the man suffer, it's the best I can do for him."

Solaina heaved an exasperated sigh. This wasn't how she'd planned on this ordeal resolving itself. Howard was supposed to do the operation, then David was supposed to leave. Simple as that! Only now she was going to do the operation and David was going to be so liquored up he'd be lucky to get out of here by morning. "I can't do this," she protested one more time, not that it was going to do any good. Howard was absolutely set on this, and the practical thought of bundling David up and taking him to Chandella for an X-ray and surgery straight away was nowhere on the agenda. He wasn't up to it yet. Even she could tell that much.

Heaving a deep sigh, Solaina went to the sink to scrub up. "Care for a cigar with your whiskey, gentlemen?" she muttered a minute later, as Howard uncapped the drinking alcohol and she uncapped the cleansing alcohol. When she'd cleaned David's wound previously, she'd used hydrogen peroxide. It worked well enough, went all bubbly and didn't particularly sting. The alcohol would work much better, but sting was an understatement. The fiery burn of the disinfectant would nearly rip his wound in half it would hurt so bad, and she was already cringing, thinking about it. Her hands were shaking, too, and her stomach churning. Next her head would go light. It always did when she found herself near a situation like this—something more than an easy patch-up.

But Howard could not do this, and she had to keep reminding herself of it. Making such a fuss over doing it herself would only remind him of the skills he'd lost, which would hurt him deeply. Victoria had told her how it depressed him. And Solaina would never hurt Howard for anything. *So just keep quiet and do it.* For Howard.

"There's still dirt in the wound," Howard said. "Under the bullet, which is why we're removing it. And I don't want him out of this bed for twenty-four hours. He's stable, but being stable doesn't mean it's time to chuck him out the door. He needs better antibiotics before we do anything with him, and overall staying here and resting is his best option."

Howard handed Solaina another package of disposable

gloves, since she'd disposed of the first ones. "Today's a lovely day for a spot of surgery, don't you think?"

At the bedside, as ready as she would ever be to do this, Solaina snapped on her gloves and took a good, hard look at David's wound. It certainly didn't seem any worse than it had earlier. If anything, it looked a tad better, which was a relief. Cleaner now, for sure. And maybe not quite so inflamed around the edges. That probably meant the peroxide had worked a little and the antibiotics were finally kicking in. Howard was correct, though. The bullet did need to come out, considering how dirty David had been when she'd first found him. Even her first effort at cleansing the wound had produced some grisly results. And heaven only knew what was still lurking about in that little hole.

All good and well, but the part where she went in after the bullet was anything but good, and she cringed again, thinking about it. No, she wasn't going to faint or do something prissy or absurdly stupid like that. But after this mess was over, she was definitely going for the whiskey.

"Are you OK with this, David?" she asked, taking a seat on the chair next to the bed in order to position herself at the same level as her operating field. *Her operating field.* Those were words she'd never heard or thought before. "With me doing the…procedure." She couldn't quite bring herself to say the "surgery."

"I think I should be the one asking you if you're OK," he replied, then tossed back his first shot of whiskey. Down in one gulp, he held out the glass for Howard to pour another. That one was gone almost as quickly as the first. "I'm not much of a drinking man any more," he said in a rather slurred voice.

Solaina looked over at Howard and gave him the nod for

one last round of anesthetic. Once David had downed that, she noted that his eyelids were drooping. Good sign. "Now or never," she whispered, then gave Howard the go-ahead to support David's ribs with a pillow. The last thing she wanted was to have him flinch or resist, and cause himself more damage. "I'm sorry about this, David. I wish you were in different hands." As she said the words, she poured the cleansing alcohol on his open wound, then sucked in a deep breath and held it, expecting a reaction from him.

His body did jerk a couple of times, and his eyes flew open and fixed on her for almost a minute, probably until the initial shock of the alcohol died down. But he didn't scream, as she'd expected. And that surprised her. Of course, David was a strong man, or he wouldn't have survived to this point. "I'm sorry," she whispered. "I wish I didn't have to…"

"Wishes don't count here," Howard interrupted. "But bullets do, and as gunshot wounds go, you've hit a bit of luck, I think. This one's a low-velocity wound, with minimal damage to the tissue, from what I could tell when I removed the bandages. Barely more than a flesh wound, and normally I wouldn't recommend doing this out here like we are, but since he's already fighting a pretty nasty infection, we need to get that controlled. So I think the best way to proceed under the circumstance is to get it clean *under* the bullet, which means it's time to get the bullet out, Solaina."

"That's it?" she asked, bracing herself for the ordeal. "Get the bullet out? That's my instruction here?"

"Go find the bullet," David slurred.

"That's it," Howard responded. "Simple operation, and it will only take a minute or two." He chuckled, raising his whiskey to his lips. "Fretting over this has already taken far longer than the procedure will."

She nodded. Biting her lower lip, she made a hasty wish on the remains of her little red-lipped Buddha, then finally reconciled herself to the task. Like it or not, she was going to have to be a nurse here, and not the kind who pushed papers for a living. "What do I do first?" she asked.

"Probe outside the wound," David responded from his inebriated stupor, then gave her a silly grin. "Guess I'm not the doctor here, am I?"

"Oh, you're the doctor," she said, feeling the muscle around the hole where the bullet was lodged. "The drunk doctor."

"Wasn't that the point of the whiskey?" he asked.

"I can't operate on a talking patient," she said as she applied gentle pressure with her gloved fingertips to the site.

"Good bedside manner," David responded, his words slurring badly now.

Solaina looked up at Howard. "What am I supposed to do about him? I don't want him talking to me, and I don't want him watching me."

"Put a pillow on his face," Howard said, smiling. "That should take care of both matters quite handily, I should think."

"What am I supposed to do about you?" she snapped at Howard, turning her attention back to David's wound. All things considered, it was small—no bigger around than her thumb. The edges were neat enough, and as she continued to probe she found a hard object under his skin. And not so far under that it should be a problem, she hoped.

Logic dictated the next step—go after the bullet. But as she picked up the package containing the sterile forceps, she looked at Howard for moral support. He merely nodded. That was it. She was on her own now. He'd passed her the figurative baton, or in this case the forceps, and the bullet was hers to remove. Drawing in a deep breath to steady her nerves, she ripped open the package, put on a pair of fresh gloves, removed the forceps from it and entered the wound site.

David stirred a little at her first probe, and muttered something she couldn't understand. He didn't thrash about, though, and she wondered if somewhere in his drunken daze he was still alert enough to co-operate, to make this easier on her. He would do that, she thought. He was a considerate man, judging from what little she knew of him. Or maybe the whiskey was working better than she'd expected.

Whatever the case, Solaina probed until she found the bullet, then grabbed it with the forceps and backed it out of the wound. In and out, it took less than a minute—probably the longest minute of her life. "Done," she said, proud of her work. A great surgeon she was not, but in this one little instance an adequate one. "It's so small," she said, taking a good look at it before she dropped it on a towel lying on the table next to the bed. So small it was no larger than the fingertip of her little finger.

"A mere toy," Howard said. "Out here they use bigger bullets than that to shoot the mosquitoes. I'd say this was a warning and not meant to be a fatality."

"Except he almost died, no matter what the size," Solaina said, cleaning the wound site with a gauze strip soaked in alcohol. "Are you OK, David?" she asked, as Howard took hold of David's wrist to feel for a pulse.

"He's dandy," Howard said. "Passed out drunk, I think. But fine. So let's get that thing cleaned out and wrapped, then go have some *naam phon-la-mai* with Victoria while David's sleeping off his binge. My poor wife has been out there on the beach all alone for much too long." Howard pulled a bottle of pills from his pocket and sat them on the table next to the bed. "Scrounged these for him on my way back through Chandella earlier. They're stronger than the ones you're giving him. Will do better on the infection in his shoulder, I should think." Then he braced David for the next shock of alcohol being poured into the wound, and chuckled when the only thing elicited was a stuporous moan. "Apparently, your friend doesn't hold his whiskey too well."

Solaina sighed as she prepared to finish up the procedure. *The surgery.* "All things considered, I think he's holding *everything* very well," she said. At this point, much better than she was, because after the wound had been dressed, and after Howard had joined his wife on the beach, Solaina sat down on the bed next to David to take a pulse, assess his respirations, make sure his wound wasn't bleeding. The last thing she remembered was how inviting the empty pillow next to him looked. "Just for a minute," she said as she laid her head down on it. "Only a minute…"

CHAPTER SIX

IT WAS dark, save for a dim light from the kitchenette, when Solaina finally opened her eyes. At first, she wasn't sure where she was. She knew she was safe. And cozy. And comfortable. She felt it, and it was such a nice feeling she didn't want to shake it off. Not just yet. Another minute, she promised herself as she snuggled in and let the feeling of pure bliss wash over her. Another minute…

She stretched out her arm and elicited a soft moan from the body next to her as it came to rest across his ribs. *A moan!*

Instantly, Solaina pushed herself away, finally realizing just where it was that she'd been feeling so safe and cozy and comfortable. In bed with him. *With David!* Curled into his side. His arm around her, and hers slung casually across him like that was the way they had always slept. With the familiarity of lovers… Instantly, she sat bolt upright, but David grabbed hold of her arm and pulled her back to him.

"Don't go," he murmured, struggling to maintain his grip as she tried to shake it off.

"I'll bet you say that to all the girls who remove bullets from your shoulder," she said, still trying to extract herself from his hold without actually hurting him. Which wasn't easy to do since he was clinging so tightly to her. Too tight for a man in his weakened condition.

"Only the girl of my dreams. Of course she doesn't want to leave me, so I don't have to beg."

Finally extracting herself from David, Solaina rolled over to the edge of the bed, then jumped up and looked around, trying to get her bearings. It was dark outside now. Well into the night, or early morning as it turned out to be when she looked at the clock.

"Howard and Victoria have gone to a hotel back up north for the night,"

"How long was I asleep?" she asked, still flustered.

"All evening, most of the night now. I didn't want to disturb you, but it's gotten to the point I can't wait any longer. You know, the call of nature. The urge to take a visit to the facility." He struggled to sit up, then slung his feet over the side of the bed. "Being dehydrated as I was, there hasn't been much of a need, but Howard made me drink a frightful amount of your *naam phon-la-mai* before he left, and now…"

"And I didn't wake up through all of that?"

"You were snoring away like a chainsaw."

"I don't snore," Solaina snapped, padding across the room to turn on a light.

David chuckled. "Well, someone I was sleeping with last night did, and Howard and Victoria will attest to that, I'm sure." He scooted toward the edge of the bed, then paused to catch his breath. "I don't suppose you could give me an assist, getting up. I think that in spite of all the *naam phon-la-mai* I've had, I'm still a little shaky. Oh, and in case I was too drunk to stammer or slur it last night, thank you for what you did. Howard said you have an aversion to those kinds of medical situations, and for you to actually do something like remove a bullet took a great amount of courage. I appreciate it, Solaina."

"You look better," she said, for a lack of a more pithy response. She *did* have an aversion, and not because she went all squeamish over such things but because she wasn't qualified to do them. But there was no point in letting on. Not now that it was over. And in some strange way it almost seemed better that he believed her to be squeamish rather than incompetent. Although if he remembered very much of the last day, he would definitely recollect her incisively clear level of nursing deficiency.

But maybe he wouldn't remember. She hoped.

"Feel better, too. And I'll feel even better if you could help me get to the…"

Solaina went around to the side of the bed from which he was attempting to stand. "Arm around my neck," she said bending over him.

"Been there," he said. "A good bit of the night. Enjoyed it very much."

"Do you want my help?" she snapped.

"Are you always so grumpy first thing in the morning? I would have pictured you much brighter. Even cheerful. Looks are deceptive, I suppose."

"Are you always so bright and cheerful in the morning?" she countered, bracing herself to help him stand. The truth be told, she was glad he was doing so much better—much better than she'd expected, actually. Which spoke well of his strength and determination. Of course, after what Howard had said about him, strength and determination were a given, and she shouldn't have been at all surprised by his speedy recovery.

The only problem was, what came next? Certainly he wasn't going to need all the nursing care she'd anticipated. A man like David wouldn't want it either. So that meant that she should probably take him somewhere—to the hospital Howard had spoken of, to a friend… She didn't know where. Then she should return to Chandella, to her own life. Close the page on this chapter.

In an ironical sense, this was a funny thing. One minute before she'd met him, she had been happily *not* involved anywhere, with anyone. And now here she was, almost dreading the minute after they parted when she would no longer be involved.

"I'm cheerful all right when I wake up with the most incredibly beautiful woman in the world in my arms. Oh, and waking up alive. That makes me almost as cheerful as waking up with you."

"If I didn't already know you were a surgeon, I'd think you were a salesman," she said, pulling him to a standing position. "Now, shift your weight onto me, Casanova, and I'll steady you as you walk across the room."

Once again, David was much stronger than she would have guessed, and what should have been a difficult maneuver turned out to be a relatively smooth walk. It was slow but steady, as David carefully measured each step he took before his foot sank into the lush Burmese carpet on the floor. "You don't need help in there, do you?" she asked, as he grabbed hold of the doorframe and took several independent steps into the bathroom.

"Depends on what kind of help you're offering."

She gave him a pert little smile. "Not the kind you're hoping for." For a moment she imagined him immersed in a nice tepid bath, with bubbles. Would David take a bubble bath? she wondered. She was in the bath with him, of course, with loofa in hand, ready to wash his back, and she could almost smell the jasmine soap.

Blinking, Solaina pushed that image out of her head and fixed on the more practical one of shutting the door and leaving David to his own devices. Not nearly as nice, but safer. *Definitely much safer,* considering how nice it had felt, waking up next to him.

"Since you're not going to be a sport about this, let's just leave it that I'll call if I need help." Grinning, he shut the door, leaving Solaina on the outside, staring at the blank door for several seconds before she turned away and hurried toward the kitchenette to make tea and figure what to do with—or without—David Gentry.

David propped himself up on the sink, panting from the exertion. *Feeling* chipper was entirely different from *looking* like he was chipper. Which he was not. But the act was for Solaina. When he walked out of her life, which would be soon, he didn't want her coming after him out of some obligation to take care of him. It would be her inclination to do just that if she thought he wasn't in good enough condition to leave. So he'd make her think that he was.

He was a pretty good actor, he thought. Solaina didn't seem overly concerned about him this morning. Of course, if she saw the way he was breathing right now—the way his chest struggled to expand and contract with each and every breath and the way his ribs challenged the movement every inch of the way— she'd tie him to the bed for sure. Solaina might resist the notion that she was a good nurse, but she was a damned good one, and he couldn't risk that element surfacing in her right now.

For her safety, of course. Being with him could make her a target, and he wouldn't have that!

First glance in the mirror, and David shook his head in disgust. He should have been better than this. Better and stronger. "Getting soft and sloppy," he murmured. To the best of his recollection he'd been wandering around in some kind of wounded state for four days now, from the start of it. Early Thursday morning, he'd made the run across the border like he'd done a hundred times before. Just a quick trip to the outskirts of Qailin to pick up a patient. A foot injury, he'd been told. Possible amputation. Probably some poor farmer stumbling onto one of the old, rusty tripwires.

He couldn't remember all the details right now, but nothing about the run had struck him as being out of the ordinary. "Except this," he murmured, running his fingers lightly over his bandaged ribs.

He was sensing a pattern. The vehicle thefts—their ambulance, their good Jeep—a supply shed robbed of extra medical equipment, broken windows in the surgery. None of it was very violent. More like warnings. Which apparently had just escalated with his broken ribs. No one had been injured before now, and this time he'd been kicked clear to the brink of death.

David raised his hand to rub his right shoulder. Coincidence? He didn't think so any more. That being the case, he had to get out of here before Solaina became a part of it. Whatever *it* was. Especially since she was running an orientation course for IMO nurses, and he wasn't ready to put IMO in the clear. He wasn't ready to accuse them either.

It just didn't make sense, he thought, splashing water in his face. Why would they come after him this way? But if not them, who?

It took David almost half an hour to wash up and make himself presentable. Smiling as he took Solaina's razor off the edge of the bathtub for a quick shave, he realised he actually wanted to make himself presentable this morning. It was the first time that urge had struck him in a good long while because outside his work, nothing else mattered. Relationships hadn't, obviously. Not after he'd gotten his second chance at medicine from Howard Brumley. And that was an opportunity he wouldn't mess up again.

He thought about Solaina as he dragged the razor over his four-day growth. With her flat-out resistance and his self-awareness… David sighed wistfully. Not meant to be. It could have been very nice, though.

"Are you cooking?" he asked Solaina a little later, as he dropped down into one of the two chairs tucked next to the chessboard-sized table.

"Not even in your dreams." Solaina laughed. "Change that to nightmares. Besides, with all the wonderful food in Dharavaj, I never cook. No domesticity in this woman. But I can do tea brilliantly. So, which do you take? Cream, sugar, lemon? Howard left some of his grog, I believe."

"Please, no. Not the grog!" He laughed. "A little sugar, lots of lemon and an ice cube. And let's just say that Howard is a much better man with spirits than I am and leave it at that."

"You don't like your tea hot?"

He gave her a suggestive grin, and a cheeky wink. "There are many things I like hot. My women, my salsa… Tea just doesn't happen to be one of them."

"I actually figured you for a soda man," she quipped lightly. "Had a bit of a think on the subject when *you* were snoring—"

"I don't snore," he interrupted, settling into place. "Must

have been some other highwayman you dragged home in the middle of the night."

Solaina laughed. "Believe me, I'm quite capable of keeping my highwaymen straight."

"So this is a regular pastime with you?"

"You're my first…"

"The words every man longs to hear."

"Simmer down, Casanova. You'll bust another rib."

"And it would be well worth the cost, if you're the one to fix it up for me."

"It's amazing what a bath will do, isn't it?" She laughed, pulling an ice tray out of the freezer and dislodging a couple of cubes from it. "One minute you're a sick, weak man and the next you're…" She shrugged. "Pretty much like every man I've ever dated."

"Handsome?" he teased.

"Randy, in spite of the most dire of circumstances." Solaina took a seat across from him and passed him a banana muffin. "And in case you were going to ask, no, I didn't bake them. I bought them in Chandella. Nice little French pastry shop just around the corner from where I live. And speaking of where I live, how is it that you know Howard?"

"Maybe I should be asking you the same question?" he countered, taking a bite of his muffin.

"We're neighbors."

"We're friends, going on ten years now. He was actually the one who got me to this part of the world and into IMO. He was lecturing in Toronto when we met, and we hit it off. Then I took a little dive off the deep end—failed marriage, muffed surgical practice—and Howard propped me up, kicked me in the seat of the pants a few times when I was determined to stay down, then eventually sent me off to Cambodia and IMO when he was a volunteer for them. It was one of those dark periods in a person's life that's best not dragged out too often." He smiled. "But I do owe Dr Brumley pretty much everything I am today. And now he volunteers at my hospital occasionally. No surgery obviously, but he's a great doctor, and we're always glad to have him when Victoria is willing to give him up for a few days."

"Well, my Howard story's not quite so dramatic. We were neighbors, he was in IMO, like you said, and he asked me to do some local orientation for the IMO nurses."

"Did he ever try recruiting you into the trenches?"

Solaina shook her head vehemently. "He knows better. Those who can't do, teach. Oh, and administrate. I can fasten a bandage brilliantly, but that's as far as practical experience goes for me. After that I let the skilled nurses step in."

"Am I hearing a bit of angst in your voice over that? Over not being a clinical nurse?"

"Not angst. More like total awareness. I made my choice years ago and I'm fine with it."

"But would you rather be doing something else?"

"Right now, I'd rather be lying outside in my cabana chair, reading a book."

"And you called me evasive." He chuckled. "You are a good nurse, you know. Very good. Good instincts…"

"Please, David, let's not go on about this," Solaina snapped. "I don't want to ruin a perfectly good muffin over it." Solaina took a sip of tea then settled into her chair. "And I'm leaving here in a while, so there's really no point in squabbling about my instincts or my skills because what they are, *or are not*, will be transferring to another hospital somewhere else."

"You're leaving?"

"That's what I do. I work for a while, then I move on. It keeps things lively in my life. I've been here two years now, which is just about my limit."

"Do you get restless?" he asked. "Is that why you leave?"

She nodded. "So far, that's the way it's worked out. And you?"

"I stay put. No wanderlust in me whatsoever. If Howard hadn't convinced me that there was a better purpose for me in Cambodia with IMO, I'd still be in Toronto, either dragging through the streets looking for my purpose or working in the family practice with my dad and my grandfather and my brother. One big, happy orthopedic lot we were."

"It sounds nice."

"In theory, it does, doesn't it?"

"Is that some angst I'm hearing in *your* voice?"

"To borrow the words of a great nurse, not angst. More like total awareness."

"Family situations can be tough," she commented. "And I'm assuming your *total awareness* is over a family situation. What about your marriage?"

"She cheated. Apparently she wanted the income and resources being married to a doctor would get her, but all the hours I was gone weren't to her liking so she found someone with better hours. Of course, I wasn't around to notice it, and she had herself quite a fling for almost three of the five years we were married before I caught on. Talk about feeling like a fool… Hell of it was, I thought we were happy, and I was just too damned caught up in my work to notice that we weren't."

"Do you still love her?"

David shook his head. "If I'd loved her like I should have, I would have noticed. But I didn't love her enough, or notice."

"My parents were apart for most of their marriage, but they were always faithful. We had a great many problems as a family, but that was the one thing we always counted on—that my parents were devoted and faithful."

"It takes a lot to be faithful," David commented dryly.

"Just love. That's all."

"The words of an optimist."

"Maybe."

"Except the optimist is out here in the middle of nowhere, alone."

"Because being out here in the middle of nowhere, alone, is what makes the optimist happy." And sad. "I live my life, David, and that's all I do. I don't involve others, don't have expectations of others, don't let others disappoint me, and I don't let others get involved. It's as simple as that. And before you go fixing some great psychological label on it, or try to diagnose my psyche, I'll answer your question before you ask it. I spent a lifetime being dominated by a man who told me who I was and what I could or could not do. So many expectations for me to be who I was not. Now I don't have that, and if the way I live seems odd, so be it. But there's no one hovering over me any more, no one telling me who I am. And when I was growing up, that was my aspiration. My only aspiration. Not to be a ballerina, or a nurse, or a teacher. I wanted to be me, however that turned out."

The bitter-sweet ring was so distinct in her voice it was all he could to keep himself from going to the other side of the table and pulling her into his arms. She needed that comfort, and he wanted to be the one to give it to her. But with the way he was drawn to her, if he did, he'd never leave. And soon he had to go. "But you're a good nurse, Solaina. No matter what you think of yourself, you have bang-up skills. Just look what you did for me."

"I did the basics—everything could have been picked up from reading a good first-aid handbook."

"That's what you think, but I think that you underestimate yourself."

"I know my skills. And what I do, I do well. Better than most, actually. But I'm not a clinical practitioner in any sense. I have the academic grasp of nursing, and the administrative ability over it, but clinical practices are for others. And that's not underestimating myself, David. That's being realistic." She huffed out an exasperated breath. "Look, I need a bath. You sit here, wait for your tea to finish chilling, have another muffin. When I'm out of the tub, we'll figure out what comes next—where you need to go, where I need to take you." Then she was off in a trot before he could say another word.

"You are good," he called after her. No matter what she thought, she was. And he truly wished he could stay around to help bolster her self-confidence, but he couldn't. "Have a nice soak, Solaina." And a nice life.

"You look bad, my friend," Matteo Carlini said as he helped David climb into the battered old Jeep. The only transportation they had left at Vista.

"Compared to what?" David muttered, stretching out in the seat.

"Compared to one of the cadavers I dissected in medical school. He had much more color than you have, and he'd been dead a year."

"He probably felt better than I do, too." The headache was setting in now. Headache, general body ache. And his heart hurt a little, too. Leaving Solaina the way he had was not nice. But he hadn't been able to think of any other way to do it. Just the act of walking out of her door had made him realize how much he hadn't wanted to go. Knowing how much he hadn't wanted to go, however, had made him realize just how much he'd needed to. Distractions brought disastrous results.

Solaina was definitely a distraction.

"So, if she was as beautiful as you described, why did you leave her bed? Another night and who knows?" Dr Matteo Carlini, a hopelessly romantic Italian surgeon, had joined David in IMO several years ago. They had become best friends in medical school, and had stayed that way.

"In case you didn't notice, I'm pretty banged up. Another night wouldn't have mattered, when it's all I can do to breathe."

"Another night always matters, Davey. Don't you forget that. So, tell me what happened. We've been worried. Sending out search parties, getting the local police ministry involved..."

"Did you get my patient out of there? The one I went after?"

"When you weren't back in twelve hours, we sent someone. We got him back, got him through surgery, and he's almost ready to go home."

"I was worried about him."

"Of course you were, but I had your back, Davey. Like you always have mine." Matteo grinned. "Although yours is in a bit of a mess right now, isn't it? But a mess I'm damned glad to see again."

"I wasn't sure, for a while, if you *would* see it again."

"Then came your angel of mercy..." Matteo shook his head. "Some men have all the luck."

"Fat lot of good it will do me."

"She's rejected you that fast? That's a record for you, isn't it?"

"No record, because I didn't even try. She's not like that." He shook his head. "I didn't even get to the place where she could reject me. She put out the warnings first thing."

"A wounded soul?"

"Aren't we all in some way?" David replied. "Besides, Solaina wants none of it with anyone. She's pretty clear about that."

"Which works out well for you since you don't trust marriage anyway."

David chuckled, then winced. "It's not the marriage I don't trust. It's the people involved."

"Yeah, yeah, I've heard it all before. And if you hadn't already taken a good whack to the head, I'd give you one, bringing that kind of an attitude around me. You know I'm a hopeless romantic, Davey. I'd marry in a minute if the right girl popped in."

"Well, Solaina's about to pop out. She's leaving Dharavaj, so there's no point in speculating about it."

"Makes it convenient, doesn't it? You're falling in love and she's leaving so you don't have to open yourself up to it again. You don't have to take that chance."

David slumped down into the seat, and shut his eyes. "Why do I keep you around as my friend?"

Matteo chuckled. "To pound some sense into your head, Davey. That's why. To tell you she's the one when you refuse to see it."

She's the one… David could almost visualize Solaina lying naked in a jasmine bubble bath. It was a fantasy to soothe the aching body, and he relaxed into it. "Well, you're right about one thing," he sighed. "If I were better at marriage, she would be the one. But I'm not, so it doesn't matter."

"You're sounding like a man in love to me. Coming from someone who's been there a dozen times, I should know the sound."

David didn't have a comeback for that because the truth was, since the first time he'd laid eyes on Solaina in Chandella, weeks ago, he hadn't thought about anyone else. And now that he'd gotten to know her, he still wasn't going to think about anybody else. Whatever that meant.

"So how does Howard fit into all this? He rang me up yesterday to tell me you were fine, and to come get you this morning, but he didn't tell me how he got involved."

"He's fatherly toward Solaina, as it turns out. They're neighbors. And I think he was surprised to find me in Solaina's bed." David chuckled. "Unconscious. Oh, and he'll be back at Vista next week. I couldn't pin him down to how long we can keep him with us this time, but he's usually good for a week." The consummate physician even in his retirement, Howard often spent days at a time at Vista. Even with his arthritic hands he was a godsend for the hospital, whatever time he gave them. "I think he wants to get us together, Solaina and me."

"He's always done that, hasn't he? Been a matchmaker? So, does he know that the one he wants to fix you up with is the one you want to be fixed up with?"

The Jeep hit a pothole, and David grabbed his ribs against the pain. "Would you slow down so the next bump you hit doesn't crack another rib?" he snapped.

"Testy, aren't you? As your personal physician, let me ask you—are you testy because you don't feel well? Or are you testy because of…? How should I put this diplomatically? You've fallen in love with the fair lady and it scares you to death as you've convinced yourself that you can't have both career and relationship? That you can do justice to one or the other, but not both?"

"Go to hell," David muttered.

Matteo laughed. "I suppose that answers my question, doesn't it? So when do I get to meet this she-devil who's taken your heart?"

"Never. I don't want her involved in this mess with the hospital, and as she's leaving Dharavaj soon…"

"And you didn't even kiss the fair lady goodbye?"

"Not even close." Unfortunately. David let out a wistful sigh as he shut his eyes, hoping to dream of Solaina for the rest of the way back.

Solaina stood on her veranda looking out at the beach. She wasn't surprised that David had disappeared. Disappointed maybe, and definitely perturbed with the way he'd chosen his exit, but she wasn't surprised.

"He doesn't do things with a great splash," Howard commented. He and Victoria had returned for the morning, having decided to stay in the area for another day before returning to Chandella. "If ever there was a young man who was focused on his work to the point of excluding just about everything else in his life, that would be our David. I saw that in him the first time I met him in Toronto. Dedicated and self-sacrificing. A good combination, especially for the kind of work he has chosen to do. Not an easy lot, though."

"And handsome," Victoria said dreamily. She was loung-ing in a cabana chair, decked out in a white, wide-brimmed straw hat and an orange and yellow flowered caftan. Victoria was a beautiful woman. Ageless, Solaina had always thought, with her flawless porcelain skin. Although Solaina knew Victoria was much closer to sixty, it took several glances at her to determine that. "I remember the first time I met him, he'd come to our flat in London for dinner. I rather fancied that I might have given him a bit of a whirl if not for the fact that Howard simply refused to leave the two of us alone." Laughing daintily, Victoria pushed back her hat and blew an adoring kiss at her husband.

"Handsome doesn't make up for rude," Solaina said. "And leaving here the way he did was certainly rude."

"He's focused on his work," Howard defended David. "Sometimes to the point that he's oblivious to everything but what he wants to see, including his marriage."

"So he told me."

"I think he loved her enough, but he loved his medicine more, and she found someone who put her first. Then he went to pieces for a while, as I would do if I'd discovered my lovely Victoria had walked out on me." He blew an adoring kiss back at his wife. "But in spite of his little misstep, David's a man who's centered on saving the world, one grain of sand at a time. He's one of the truly good ones, dear. And a man who's learnt his lesson, in case you're interested."

Solaina ignored that last comment. He meant well every time he tried to fix her life. That was simply part of Howard, and her usual response was to smile patiently on the outside, bite her tongue on the inside. "So why did you recruit him to IMO?"

Howard chuckled. "Not recruited so much as persuaded. I

spotted him as the right type and talent for the hard work, with the essential devotion that it takes. He wasn't happy in the family practice, he was struggling in his life, and more than anything he needed a change at the precise time I was setting up the unit in Cambodia. The rest, as they say, is history."

"History is right," Solaina muttered. "And that's what Dr David Gentry is, as far as I'm concerned. *History!*"

Howard chuckled again. "With the way that young man was looking at you when you weren't watching him…and the way that you're overreacting to such a simple thing as him leaving…that's not history, dear. I think it could be the future. And a very interesting one indeed. *If you allow it.*"

"And after you've had that whirl with David that my dear Howard deprived me of years ago, you'll simply have to tell me every detail," Victoria exclaimed. "Every last, luscious detail of it." She turned to her husband, and tilted back her hat to expose her face. "You wouldn't mind, would you, dear?"

Howard strolled over to Victoria, bent and placed an affectionate kiss on her cheek. "As if you would, dear."

Howard and Victoria had carried in a hamper stuffed with delicious food—breads and biscuits, fruits, caviar, smoked oysters, cheese, all accompanied by a nice selection of wine. The wine Solaina declined because she would be motoring back to Chandella shortly. But she stuffed herself on the rest of the delicacies until she couldn't even force herself to top the meal with a wonderful little chocolate truffle. Then she said her goodbyes to the couple, promising to join them for dinner in a few days.

Once they were gone, on their way to spend another day at a resort up the coast, Solaina followed them along the highway until she came to the spot where she'd met David. Stopping, she got out and walked slowly across to the place where he'd lain on the ground, then bent down and ran her fingers over the dirt there. "Howard speaks so highly of you," she whispered. "That's high praise. What is it about you, David Gentry, that attracts Howard, that attracts Victoria, and most especially attracts me?"

Yes, he was handsome, and she liked handsome. But looks were not a factor she'd ever weighed too heavily in any matter. And he was blond, and admittedly she did have a certain fascination for blonds. But once more that really was not a fact of any merit in all this, since she had no intention of an involvement any more than she already had.

"Is it your reputation, David? The fact that you've dedicated your life to a higher cause? Or that you actually picked yourself up and started all over again?" Something she hadn't been able to do after Jacob.

"These are all such weighty things," she said, righting herself and brushing the dirt off her hands. Weighty, indeed. But when she thought of David, she thought in terms of…happiness.

Yes, happiness. In spite of what they'd gone through together, and in spite of his rather odd social skills, she'd liked taking care of him, liked talking to him even when he'd been delusional. Liked looking at him when he'd been sleeping. So, yes, in a sense she had not expected from all of this, David had made her happy. And she missed him. "Two days, Laina, and you've gone all soft and gooey over him. You run him over with your car, then take him to your bed, and now look at you, forgetting everything you stand for." What she stood for…a solitary life.

Just look at her, indeed! The instant Solaina climbed back

into her car, she made a U-turn in the road and headed back in the direction from which she'd just come. Only she passed the turn-off to her cottage and drove south for another thirty minutes until she reached the turn-off for a road that would take her straight to Kantha.

"So, what are you going to do once you get there?" she asked herself as she contemplated making the turn. "Because either way you go, there's probably no going back." Was it back to the hospital to finish up her job then start over someplace else? Or on to seek out David and whatever it was he did out there in the jungle, just because…well, she wasn't sure why. And maybe that was a reason to go after him. To find out why.

Solaina took a deep breath, looked both ways up and down the highway, then made the turn. Maybe the biggest turn of her life.

CHAPTER SEVEN

VISTA HOSPITAL was a tidy little facility sitting some way out of the tiny town of Kantha. Perched atop a modest hill overlooking a rubber plantation, it was neither a noticeable place nor an obscure one. Vista blended perfectly into the landscape—its natural wood-frame timbers in harmony with its environment, its giant rhododendron bushes and arrow-straight bamboo trees like everything else the eye could see for miles around.

From Kantha on over to Cambodia, an area David could navigate in his sleep—or, if necessary in a delirious stupor—the climate was hotter, and wetter, than the rest of Dharavaj. Or in the rest of the entire southeast region, for that matter. David preferred the cooler climes of Toronto, but he did love the lush jungle greens that came with the rainforest.

Resting on the front porch of the hospital, his feet propped up on a stool and drinking the soda Solaina had accused him of preferring over tea—which he did—he chuckled, thinking about his daft ramblings of late—deciduous trees and evergreens and the ever-fabulous rhododendron. Certainly that would have made no sense to Solaina, but it made all the sense in the world to him. That had merely been his mind fighting to stay alert, focusing on the things he knew, the things he loved. And right now, looking out over the vista, he was reminded of how much he loved this place—its vast beauty as well as its dark side.

If someone were to tell him he would spend the rest of his life here, he wouldn't complain about it. Even though he might mutter a bit about the heat.

"It grows on you, doesn't it?" Matteo said, stepping up behind him.

"You don't know how much until you think you might never see it again."

"You scared the hell out of me, Davey. After a couple of days, we got a rumor up here that you'd been killed."

"And if I had, you'd have made a fine director here," David said blandly. His mind wasn't on the hospital yet, or on work either. It was on Solaina, and he wasn't ready to turn off those thoughts and go back to the real world. Another minute or two was all he needed. Just a minute or two, then he'd put her aside and step back into the life he'd chosen.

"Still going all melancholy over her?" Matteo asked.

David shook his head, trying to shake off the feeling. Matteo was right about the melancholia, but he wasn't about to let him know. "Just tired. And sore."

"She did a good job on your shoulder. Couldn't have done better myself. It's clean. Your labs came back normal, and your white count's fine. She saved your life, Davey. And you're doing remarkably well so early on after that kind of a trauma."

Matteo had changed the dressing, too, then X-rayed his ribs. Except for the fact that they still hurt, and he *was* still fairly incapacitated, he was doing remarkably well. "Do you believe in fate?" he asked.

"You've got it bad, haven't you?" Matteo asked.

"A lot worse than I intended. But I'll get over it."

"Or not."

"She runs away. She's got it in her head that she's not good enough, and I think she runs away from it. And I've done all my running. That pretty much says everything that needs to be said."

Matteo laughed. "Or not."

David spun around and jabbed his old friend in the arm. "I think I must still be loopy, talking to someone like you about all this."

"Ah, but I am still a romantic at heart, Davey. My relationships may not be the lasting kind you're mooning over with this Solaina right now, but at the moment they're intense."

"Believe me, we never even came close to intense, let alone moony." Although when he'd woken up to find her sleeping in his arms, the feelings that had run through him then had been more intense than anything he'd ever felt in his life. "I ruined her little holiday, and I think she resented that from the start." He chuckled. "Can't blame her on that one, though. She was out for some time alone with a romance novel, and what I brought her was anything but romance."

"The question is, did she want romance?"

"She wanted peace and quiet."

"Did you dent her car when you ran into it?" Matteo asked. "Maybe you should go back there, have a good look, make reparations if necessary." He grinned. "And I'm not talking about financial reparations here. Maybe something more in keeping with that book she was reading?"

"Maybe I should go catch up on some of the charts while you actually do some work."

"Oh, so the boss returns with a whip and a vengeance. What are you going to do? Dock my pay if I mess about out here another few minutes? So tell me, how *would* you go about taking something from nothing?"

David laughed. Matteo had an irreverent way about him that always caused David to perk up when he needed it. Of course they didn't get paid much for this. The hospital funding was adequate from various humanitarian sources, but the best they could, or would, manage was a living stipend. And that did not translate into living at the high end. A private room, food, and pocket change for the necessities. That was it.

But Matteo had known that, coming in. So had David. And neither of them would have made a change for anything. "I'm sorry you were worried about me," he said. "There were a few times I was pretty worried about me, too. And now that we don't have the Hummer, I don't know what we're going to do for transport."

"Somebody wants us out of here," Matteo said, concern registering on his face. "Don't know why, exactly. Could be personal, but I don't think that I've offended any woman enough lately that her husband would come after us. Could be professional, but I just don't see IMO turning into an arch-enemy over some turf dispute. We're on the same side. We just go about our duties differently. Maybe they are prickly about the whole matter of losing us." He thought about it for a moment, then shook his head. "Nah. That can't be it. It was six months ago now, and I don't know why they'd still be taking it so badly they'd come after the hospital, and you. Unless they want to shut us down so they can get you—or all three of us—back. You, me and Howard."

"If they wanted me back, they wouldn't shoot me. Who's in charge now? I haven't kept up."

"They took on some business genius named Léandre. He's going to take them in that new direction they want to go."

The direction that had caused David, Howard and Matteo to leave. The one that was so much about bottom lines and expenditures and things that weren't the grass-roots cause David admired. Maybe the business emphasis was necessary. IMO was growing and fiscal responsibility was certainly a part of it. As a director of a small hospital, he knew that. But the bottom line should never replace care and concern, and when IMO had announced that it was cutting back its operation in Cambodia because of finances, and that it would soon start evaluating the patients based on need, that's when he'd known it had been time to leave. As far as he was concerned, if they came to him, they had a need. The rest of it didn't matter.

He didn't fault IMO for their change. They were a large international organization now, and to spread themselves all about the globe perhaps the changes were necessary. But on a personal level he didn't agree with the changes. Which was why he'd left. The Cambodia unit needed its experienced doctors. But the plans had been to pull them out and send them away, no matter what—him to an administrative position, Howard to retirement, and Matteo to who knew where.

It had been a done deal by the time he'd been called in on it. Howard's exit papers processed, after all the man had done for them, David's transfer papers ready... A shabby way to treat volunteers, so he'd spouted off—in retrospect, more than he should have—then had left. Yet he had a hard time believing that their new business guru would have it in for him or his hospital. "Never met him, never heard of him. And if IMO is behind the sabotage, what would be in it for them other than to prove that they're right? It's not about egos after all."

"If not IMO, Davey, then who?"

David shrugged with his one good shoulder. "Coincidence, maybe. Unrelated events piling up on us."

"But you wouldn't run out, would you?" Matteo asked, suddenly serious. "Now that you've been attacked?"

"It makes me more determined to stay, actually. We're doing a good thing here, and I'm not budging from this place."

"Even for the lovely Solaina?"

David sighed wistfully. "Unfortunately, even for the lovely Solaina, if she would have me. Which she wouldn't."

"And we're right back to you going all moony over her." Matteo patted his friend on the shoulder. "You're hopeless, Davey."

"Well, for once we agree."

"So, what do we tell the authorities about your last little fracas?"

"Same thing we told them before. Don't know who, don't know why. And when the regional minister writes up his report, it will get filed away with the rest of them, under the sign of the great big question mark."

"This one needs to stay at the top of the stack," Matteo said. "Vandalism is one thing, but what they did to you…"

David sighed. "Look, I'm tired. It's been a rough few days."

"And as your physician, I prescribe bed rest. *Alone.*"

"I should argue with you, and insist on doing some work

around here to help you get caught up. But for once you're right. I should rest."

"I'm right?"

"Just this once," David said, as he dragged himself back inside Vista and into his own little room.

"Where am I now?" Solaina muttered, stopping her car to take a look at her surroundings. Not that having a good look around mattered, since she'd never been here before. "Kantha has got go be around here," she said, walking to the rear of her car, as if that would make a difference in what she would see.

And if she did see Kantha from there, or David's hospital, what then?

Honestly, she didn't know. "Hello, David. I just happened to be in the neighborhood, so I thought I'd stop in and say hello." He wouldn't believe that, even if he was delirious again. "I think I'm lost." That much was the truth, but unless Chandella had moved to the other side of the country, there was no reason to be lost in these parts. "Here's a bill for the dent in my car." Good one, and if she tried, she could probably kick a dent right in the spot where he'd run into her.

Solaina slumped down over the top of her car and moaned. This was a silly notion any way she played it out. She wasn't sure why she was chasing after him, wasn't sure why she wasn't turning back, wasn't sure why she wasn't going forward. "Make up your mind," she muttered, wondering if banging her head on the car might bang some sense into herself.

Here she was, standing on the bank of the Kantha River, looking across at the Church of the Immaculate Conception. A beautiful church with fine architectural detail, and quite a surprise out here. One of the locals, a young boy of about ten, had pointed her in this direction over an hour ago, promising her it was the fastest way to get to the hospital. Then he'd held out his cute, grubby little hand, expecting payment for his directions. Solaina obliged, naturally. How could she not?

The boy had said the hospital was up on the hill, that she would see it from the overlook when she saw the church. Which she hadn't, of course. Then she'd driven to the next overlook, and the one after that. And now, five overlooks later, she was about to resign herself to the notion that David Gentry had been a figment of her tired imagination all along, and his hospital called Vista, in the town called Kantha, simply did not exist.

"OK, David. Where are you?"

She turned slowly, taking in every vantage point for the last time. If she couldn't find it this time, she was going to go back to Chandella and forget this whole weekend had ever happened. Out of sight, out of mind, out of memory.

One more full sweep of the area and nothing came into view, so Solaina went back to the car door, preparing to get in and admit her mistake in coming here. But as she twisted around to sit down, she spotted something far off in the distance. It was indeed on a hill, as the boy had said, and overlooking practically all of the tiny town below it. And so hidden she wondered if it was even meant to be seen. "Guess I'll go give it a look," she said. She had come this far after all. What was one more dead end?

Thirty minutes later, and one bumpy roadway after another, Solaina finally arrived. VISTA the sign over the door read. Not Vista Hospital, not in a native language. Just plain VISTA. And that it was. The view was spectacular.

Out of the car, Solaina paused for a moment to capture the full essence, then she headed up to Vista's main door, not quite sure what she'd find, or even what she should expect to find.

What she found, however, was a tiny yet modern little hospital, looking pretty much the way any hospital on the outskirts of Kantha should look. Neat, clean, something that might have been more appropriate to the 1950s. She was actually impressed. Somehow she'd expected something more in the way of a jungle hut, with a thatched roof and no doors.

"May I help you?" a kind-faced woman asked. Cambodian, Solaina guessed.

"I'm here to see David Gentry."

"Dr Gentry is resting. He's not well. Would Dr Carlini do?"

Solaina hadn't pictured David here with another doctor. The image was of David alone, slaving over his work twenty-four hours a day. But as she watched two more people in green surgical scrubs cross the hall, she realized this was a well-staffed facility, and David might actually be one of several doctors. "I'll talk to Dr Carlini," she said.

A handsome Italian appeared several minutes later and grabbed her hand in a hearty shake. "Matteo Carlini," he said, grinning from ear to ear. "And what may I do to help you?"

"My name is Solaina…"

"*The* Solaina?" he asked, giving her a good, hard once-over, then smiling his approval.

She nodded, glancing down self-consciously at her shorts, then looking back up at him and smiling. "Yes, I'm *the* Solaina, if that's in reference to David. Solaina Léandre."

Matteo whistled. "Now, that's something I didn't expect to hear."

"I'm sorry?"

"Believe me, from where I'm standing there's absolutely nothing to be sorry about. At least, I don't think there is." He shook his head, then grinned. "Let me go get Davey for you."

"If he's sleeping, I don't want to disturb him."

"Trust me, he's already disturbed."

Matteo scrambled off down the hall while Solaina leaned against the wall and waited. And watched. She couldn't see the patient wards, but as someone whose job it was to evaluate staff, the staff here was excellent in everything she could see. Professional-looking, professional-acting, not loitering, no idle chatter. Even though she couldn't see their work, they would have certainly passed muster in their ancillary particulars, and normally when that happened, the work was exemplary.

David was a lucky man to be working here at Vista, she decided.

"What do you mean, she's here?" David mumbled, not even opening his eyes.

"I mean here. Outside, in the waiting area. Waiting!"

"She's in Chandella by now."

"Long legs—the kind that make you ache all over from wanting them. The most beautiful black hair I've ever seen. Black eyes. She has a hint of an accent—French or Haitian. Couldn't tell which."

"She's here?" David gasped.

"Wake up, Davey. She's not only here, she's looking for you. Lucky man!"

David pulled himself up to the side of his bed. "Did she say what she wants?"

"No, nothing like that. But she did say something pretty damned interesting."

"What?"

"Her last name."

Frowning, David tried to dredge it up. "Back in Chandella I only heard her first name, and when I was with her…" He started to push himself up out of the bed, but Matteo laid a hand on his shoulder and forced him to stay there.

"Think you'd better stay down for this one."

"What?"

"Her last name. You definitely don't want to be standing for it."

"Just tell me what her name is," he snapped.

Matteo grinned, then took a step backwards. "Léandre. Her name is Solaina Léandre."

David groaned, dropping his head into his hands. "It's a co-incidence, right?"

"If you say it over and over, maybe that'll make it so."

"It's a coincidence," David repeated, although he was already connecting the dots mentally. They were all connecting now into one great big picture that looked like IMO.

"Judging from the rather unpleasant look on your face, I'd say you've gone and fallen in love with…well, she could be the enemy, now, couldn't she?" Matteo commented, smiling. "And it's rather likely that she is."

"Let's just say I've fallen into *something*, and I'm not sure what it is."

"I'd suggest that, instead of wasting time here with me, you go out there and ask her. Because if you don't…"

"Five minutes. I need to splash some water on my face, put on a clean shirt…"

"Three minutes, then I'm bringing her in here. The rule of the game, Davey, is that you never, ever, leave a lady like Solaina standing alone for five minutes."

As soon as Matteo shut the door behind him, David struggled over to the sink, dragged a cold, wet rag over his face and looked at himself in the mirror. It was all the same—same cuts and bruises, same tired expression. But now there was a worried look added to the mix. Worried because she was here. Worried because her name was Léandre. Worried because he wasn't sufficiently convinced that IMO *wasn't* behind this string of assaults. Just plain worried all the way round, but most of all because of the feelings he had for Solaina. It would have been so much easier if she'd gone back to her world and left him to his.

But he was very glad she hadn't. One more meeting with the lovely Solaina was worth everything.

David headed to the door into the hall, stopped, took in a deep breath and braced himself. "She's not the enemy," he whispered. At least, not until proven guilty.

Not an enemy to his heart. And that was the real problem.

"It's a beautiful view from here," Solaina said, gazing out over the valley below the hospital. It was late now, and the gentle pinks and golds of dusk were settling over the jungle. "A nice place for a hospital." She spun around to David, who was still standing in the doorway. "Why did you leave the way you did?"

"I had to get back."

She studied him for a moment. He was rigid, she thought. Not nervous, not necessarily in pain, but definitely not comfortable. This was not the David she'd spent the last couple of days caring for. Something about his delirium had made him rather loose and charming. And bits and pieces of David had popped out all over the place when he'd been ill. But now? *What had happened to him?* "That's it? You had to get back? I think a goodbye might have been in order. I was worried about you."

"You were in the bath. I didn't want to disturb you."

"So you did, what? Call your friend to come get you?"

"Howard made the call, actually. To let everybody here know I was safe. And he arranged to have Matteo come and fetch me today, when I was up to the trip back here. I just didn't want to be any more of an inconvenience about this than I already was, Solaina. And you were put out, having me there. You can't deny it."

"Inconveniencing me is about removing a bullet from your shoulder and, believe me, you have no idea how that inconvenienced me. As far as being put out by having you there, yes, I suppose I was a little. I got over it, though, and rather enjoyed having the company for a change. But you letting me know you were leaving was not an inconvenience, David. It was a basic civility that, quite honestly, I expected from you." She turned away from him to look back over the valley. It had been silly to come here. She'd known that at the start of the journey and now, at the end, he was emphasizing that. It was quite clear he didn't want her here, and if she couldn't tell it from the bristly set of his body, she certainly could from the ice-cold tone in the few words he had spoken to her. She didn't belong here; he didn't want her here. "I'm sorry for bothering you," she said, stepping off the porch and contemplating a dead run straight to her car to spare herself any further humiliation.

What had she thought, coming here anyway? She, who didn't do romance, had been caught up in a moment. In a fantasy. And the price was total embarrassment. She deserved it, of course. Let your guard down, and look what happened. She and David weren't friends now, and they weren't going to be friends. She should have let it go when he'd walked away. Patch him up and set him free.

Before she was ten steps off the porch, David caught up with Solaina and grabbed her arm. "I didn't expect to see you here," he panted, so winded he actually leaned heavily into her for support.

"No, I suppose you didn't, since you did not tell me where here was."

"But you found me."

"Only because you babbled about Kantha when you were feverish. And Howard did mention your hospital. It's not easy to find, David. I asked ten people in town before I found one little boy who knew where you are. It took me hours."

"We have one purpose…"

"Landmine victims," she confirmed.

"And it's a bit ticklish because we are bringing people over the border. The Dharavaj government is very gracious, but the fact remains that some of these people…most of these people don't have visas that allow them into the country so, in essence, we're smuggling them in." He paused to breathe. "I need to sit…"

Taking a firm hold of him around the waist, Solaina grumbled, "You need to be in bed, so put your arm up over my shoulder."

By the time they'd taken the few steps back to the porch, he was almost a dead weight on her. His legs were moving, but the bulk of him was upright only because of her strength.

"Just sit down in the chair," she snapped, "and I'll go get your friend, Matteo."

"I don't need him," David gasped, sinking cautiously onto the wooden deck chair. "I'm fine."

"You're as stubborn as a mule," she snapped, stooping to help him position his legs.

"And you're not?" He laughed. "Of course, on you stubborn's becoming."

"I shouldn't have come here," she said, looking up at him. "It was a mistake that I won't make again. But you owe me one thing before I leave, David. You owe me an explanation."

They were so close, mere inches from each other, that she could feel the gentle heat radiating from his body. Gentle heat now, not a raging fever. And they were no longer nurse and patient; they no longer shared the intimacy that nursing a person back to health entitled her to. So she stepped back from him. "Why did you leave me like you did? To worry? You owed me better than that."

"You're leaving Dharavaj, Solaina. You don't need to be tangled up with whatever kind of mess it is that I've got going."

"That's not it, David. You don't lie well." She could see it in his eyes, hear it in the tone of his words.

"That's part of it. Honestly. I don't know what this is and I really don't want you involved."

"And the other part. The *real* reason?"

"Because I have feelings for you, Solaina." He took a deep breath, then frowned. "You wanted honesty. Here's more. I imagined you in a role I couldn't put you in. And a role you didn't want to be put in. So I left before it got out of hand."

At least he was honest. More so than she'd ever expected.

"You're supposing that I would have let you get that close." She might have, though. She probably would have. Frightening thought that it was, her guard had been coming down with David from the first moment she'd heard him babble on about the trees, and part of her was glad he'd had enough of his guard up for both of them, because hers was temporarily out of order. "And you were merely saving me from you?"

David chuckled. "It seems that way, doesn't it? I can't do justice to a relationship, and you don't want to try."

"But that's supposing a relationship exists between us."

"And I *was* supposing a relationship. From the first moment I opened my eyes and there you were, that's all I could think about. All I could think about after I got back here. And, like it or not, that *is* a relationship, Solaina. One I couldn't draw you into, so I left. Believe me, everything in me wanted to get involved."

"And that just about says it all, doesn't it?" She drew in a deep, shuddering breath, then shook her head. "You know, I really shouldn't have come here," she murmured, stepping away from him. "And I won't again." She'd just been rejected in something she was fighting so hard against. It was humiliating, and she was hurt in spite of the fact that David was correct. She didn't want this between them. So how stupid was it that she was feeling this way when she should be thanking him right now? Wishing him well. Walking away with what she truly wanted.

But somehow she felt utterly miserable.

She'd made a wrong turn on the road to Kantha, and now it was time to turn back.

"I'm glad you're doing well, David." Solaina extended her

hand to him. "I don't expect we'll cross paths again, so I suppose this is goodbye."

He took her hand and held it for a second. "I'm glad you did come," he whispered. "Even though I'm so conflicted about this, I wanted to see you again, almost from the moment I left you. And I apologize for not doing that better. You deserved better, Solaina. When I say that I can't get involved with you, that's the truth. I can't. But that doesn't mean I don't want to, because that's all that I want. Which is the reason I can't. If that makes any sense to you." He smiled, then leaned forward and kissed the back of her hand. "So will you forgive me for hurting you, pretty lady? Because I'd rather crack another rib than do that."

Solaina drew in a ragged breath. She was leaving, David was staying. So there was no destiny involved here, and she simply had to keep her head about that. "David, this—"

Before her words were out, he stood up and pulled her into his arms. There, locked in his embrace, battling with surrender and yet still contemplating retreat, the feel of his lips on hers came as a shock—not so much because she hadn't expected the kiss but because she hadn't known how much she'd wanted it.

And as his tongue stole into her mouth, brushing over hers, taunting it playfully and begging for her response, Solaina finally set aside her doubts and questions and gave herself over to the moment. But *only* the moment.

Lifting her hand, she slipped it around his neck and ran her fingers through the scraggly blond hair brushing across his collar, delighting in the demanding force of his jaw as he journeyed from her mouth to trace his lips down the contour of her chin then lower, to her throat. Like the pouring of sweet, golden honey, it was slow and deliberate, as though he was savoring every tingling inch of her flesh.

And her flesh did tingle so deliciously wherever he touched it.

David breathed deeply, and a muted growl rumbled deep inside his throat. Then he pulled away—abruptly. Much sooner than she'd expected. Much sooner than she'd wanted. And even in the fading light of the day, she saw that he regretted what had just happened. "It doesn't matter," she said, raising her hand to her lips. Already they were swollen, and she knew if the light was better he would see the scarlet of her cheeks and the keen disappointment in her eyes. Because she *was* disappointed and, yes, even embarrassed. But mostly disappointed.

"It matters more than you know," he rasped.

"We are what we are," Solaina said. "And there's no getting around it, is there?" She stepped off the porch, then turned back to David. "I'm glad you're better. And I wish you well here at Vista." This wasn't the way she'd wanted it to end, but maybe it was for the best. Foolish notions didn't have a place in her life, and David was a foolish notion. A foolish, romantic notion. "Goodbye, David," she said as she picked up her pace to her car.

She wasn't returning to her cottage tonight—the long trip back to Chandella would allow her ample time to get over this silliness. Besides, the cottage would call back her brand-new memories of David and remind her of how slow-witted she'd just been. And if there was one thing Solaina didn't require, it was a reminder.

"Wait, Solaina," David called. He stepped off the porch, but buckled over before he could run to her.

She turned around in time to see David crumple over, and her first impulse was to go back to him, to help him to his bed, which was where he rightfully belonged. But this was a hospital, and there were others here infinitely more qualified to take care of him than she was. Infinitely more qualified and infinitely less confused. So she continued to her car, and when she arrived she took one more look, only to see David sinking to his knees in the dirt. "Damn," she muttered, running back to him. "Why do you keep doing this to me? Letting me get only so far, then pulling me back to you?"

"Because you have an uncanny way of being in the wrong place for you at the right time for me," he grunted, as she helped him stand.

"Or because you have an uncanny way of *collapsing* in the wrong place for me at the right time for you." He was leaning heavily into her, not at all averse to letting her support him. "Are you bleeding?" she asked. "Your shoulder?"

"Don't think so," he grunted.

"Your ribs?"

"The same."

"Can you stay here while I go get someone to help get you inside? Because right now you shouldn't be walking."

"Think I might collapse again."

"Then lean on me, David. It's only a few steps." And a proximity to him that was much closer than anything she wanted ever again. But he was, after all, still her patient in a farfetched sense of the word, she supposed. Once she delivered him back inside to his friend Matteo, though, it was over. For good!

CHAPTER EIGHT

"So I told her I couldn't get involved, but that I wanted to get involved, then I kissed her and she left, and I went after her…"

"And I'm surprised she waited around after all that, but she said she wanted to, until I finished examining you. She's in the waiting room, although I can't promise you how long she'll stay after that merry-go-round you've put her on. Once she hears that you're fine, I think she'll leave. With good cause." Matteo looked down at David, sprawled out on his bed, and shook his head skeptically. "That was the most pitiful acting job I've ever seen, by the way."

"Meaning what?" David snapped.

"Meaning that deliberate fall to your knees. You looked like a centenarian with gout, getting down to the ground the way you did. You're lucky she didn't back over you."

"It wasn't an act. I feel like a centenarian with gout."

"Then maybe you should have groveled a little while you were down there. The kiss was good, though. I think she might have enjoyed it. But to shove off like you did, and in the middle of it? She should have backed over you *twice* for that one."

"And exactly how much *weren't* you watching?"

Matteo chuckled. "I always figured it was bound to happen to you, but you don't have much of a knack for it, do you? And I'm betting you didn't ask her about the Léandre connection either."

David pushed himself up to a sitting position, holding his breath against the pain. "So what if I didn't?"

"You're pitiful. That's what. You're so crazy in love with the girl you're afraid to find out the truth about her, afraid to get tangled up with her, afraid to let her go, afraid to—"

"OK, I get the point."

"And the point is sappy, old friend. Which makes me very happy for you, if you can get it worked out, because this time you'll know better than to ignore her. As if you could. Solaina's not the kind of lady a man can ignore. Oh, and as you're figuring out how to make things right between you two, see if she's connected to IMO in ways other than the obvious. How much? And how is she related to this other Léandre who's in charge now, and is he the one behind the sabotage?"

"Well, that will just make things spiffy between us, won't it? I love you, but I can't because I'm an emotional mess over my past failures. Oh, and by the way, did someone in your family try to kill me?"

"When you put it that way, you're right. I think you're going to need a little more than spiffy here," Matteo quipped.

"Just send her in, will you?" David snapped. "And don't spy on us this time. OK? Let me humiliate myself without the public display and commentary afterwards."

"The object of the kiss, Davey, boy, is to keep her there, not send her running. Just keep that in mind next time you get the urge." Matteo was still chuckling on his way out the door, while David was doing some mental head-banging on the wall.

So, what had all that been about anyway? For sure, the kiss had been an accident, and ending it when he had done had been rude, but probably the wisest thing to do, as he shouldn't have been kissing her in the first place. "Stupid," he muttered. "Let me count the ways." Ways he didn't want to think about. Ways in which he was falling so hard for Solaina Léandre he couldn't even think straight any more.

"Matteo said you're fine?" Solaina took only a few steps into David's room before she stopped.

Her demeanor was cold, her arms folded across her chest. Protecting herself, probably. And who could blame her, after everything he was putting her through?

"He said something about you being overcome by exhaustion, that your ribs are fine and your shoulder hasn't ripped open again. And he asked me to stay until the exam was finished. He said you were begging me to."

David fought back a grin. Good old Matteo. Ever the romantic. And the consummate liar when it was necessary.

"I just wanted to apologize to you one more time. And say thank you for helping me. And he was right. It was only exhaustion." That was no lie either. He *was* tired, and thinking about it made him want to go back to Solaina's bed to rest.

"Then I should get going. It's a long trip, and I have to be back in Chandella by morning." She still hadn't come all the way into the room. Not even far enough to close the door behind her, and she was already backing away from him. *Uncomfortably.*

"Solaina," he said. "Stay here. Just tonight. I know you're afraid of the way I feel and, to be honest, so am I. But I want just one more night. Besides, it's too far to go, and it's so late now. The roads can get dangerous at night if you're not familiar with them." This was definitely awkward between them; the tension was so thick in the room it was practically sucking the oxygen right out. "You can stay in the guest quarters."

"David, I can't. I've really got to go home, back to my real life. I appreciate the offer, but this little back and forth we've got going between us won't work. I don't know what it is, and I don't want to know what it is. And you don't either, which is why you left the cottage the way you did this morning." She shrugged. "You keep things simple in your way, and I keep them simple in mine. It works out, and sometimes it works out by running away. Apparently, for both of us."

"You do scare me," he admitted. "When I came to, out there on the road that night, and saw you…" He shook his head. "You scare me because I want to know everything, Solaina. Everything about you. Who you are, where you come from, what makes you who you are."

"Why, David? What's the point? I tell you mine, you tell me yours, then where does it get us, besides another step closer to not understanding what we're doing? Hey, if it's sexual, I can deal with that. If it's intellectual, I can deal with that. But we've put ourselves off limits to each other, which makes it all the more tempting. And I don't understand that kind of temptation because, honestly, I'm never tempted. Not until I met you."

She hesitated in the hallway outside the door. "I don't want to understand it because it comes with all kinds of expectations, and expectations only lead to disappointment. I really don't want more disappointment, David. Or more expectations of me."

Two more steps and she would be out of his sight. Then out of his life. Once she left, she would not return. "But why does it have to lead to disappointment, Solaina? Is that what you expect from all your relationships?"

She smiled sadly. "You yourself have this same conflict, don't you? You want a relationship, but you can't have it because you think one failure sets your path. Isn't that already a disappointment?"

"More than you know."

"We're strangers, David, and that's the way we should leave it."

"But do you want to leave it that way, Solaina?" he asked, not sure why, except he knew that, deep down, he didn't want them to part as strangers. Aside from the physical attraction—and admittedly, he'd never been as powerfully attracted to another woman as he was to Solaina—there was something about her that drew him in all the way. "As strangers? We met as strangers and part as strangers? Is that what you really want from this?"

Solaina laughed. "You know, just before you ran out into the road, I was fashioning a mental image of the man I'd like to meet someday. It was you, David. Believe it or not, right down to the roots of your hair, it was you. At least, in looks. I hadn't gotten past that part, though, because in truth I've never gotten past that. That's where it stops for me, and there's never been any point in going further because I always move on. Which is what I'm doing now. Moving on."

"Because you haven't found what you're looking for?"

"Because I haven't been looking. You said you wanted to know me, and that's me, David. Solaina Léandre, always passing through on her way to another destination."

That was the first time he'd heard her say her last name, and it caused his breath to catch. A much harder catch than he'd expected, considering his suspicions. Here he was with so many complications between them, yet he was practically begging her to stay.

"One evening, Solaina. That's all I want. One evening where I'm not the patient and you're not my nurse. You can stay on that side of the room, next to the door, ready to pass through it and run away any time you feel the need, and I'll stay here and hope that you don't. And we'll talk. Try to figure out what this is, what we can do about it…"

"Why, David?"

"Because you feel it as much as I do. And I think you're honest enough to admit it. Otherwise why would you have come after me?"

Solaina took two steps back toward his door, but still didn't enter the room. "Out there that night on the road, you said you were glad I was the one who found you, that you'd dreamt I would come for you. And you mentioned me by name. You also said I smelt of jasmine just like the last time." She finally crossed the threshold. "At the time I didn't pay much attention because you were delirious, and I was busy, trying to take care of you. But now it's time to be honest with me. You know me, don't you? Before that night, you knew me."

He shook his head. "Not in the sense that we'd actually met."

"So what is it?"

"I saw you once, in the hospital. You were directing a group of nurses, giving them instructions. And I stopped for a minute to watch you." *And fall in love.*

"And in your delirium you recognized me? You had a concussion, you were dehydrated, infected and dying. How could you possibly remember me?"

Because the heart never forgets, pretty lady. The heart

never forgets. Such a simple explanation, and one she couldn't hear. "I suppose the mind does strange things under duress."

"I suppose," she said. "But it does seem like such an odd coincidence, doesn't it?"

Coincidence—that word again. And another coincidence… "Are you related to Bertrand Léandre?" he asked, completely out of the blue. She stiffened immediately under the question, and from her response he already knew the answer.

"He's my father. Why?"

"Since you're with IMO in a sense, and since he's taken over as head of the board of directors…"

"What?" she gasped.

She seemed genuinely surprised. Actually, shocked was a much better word. So, was she acting, or hadn't she known? "Your father—he's the director of IMO now. Has been for several weeks, ever since—"

"Davey," Matteo yelled, running up behind Solaina, "we've got six people on their way in. All victims, all in pretty bad shape. They're coming in with International Rescue, and they've radioed ahead that they're halfway up the hill to us already. They're about ten minutes out."

David dropped his legs over the side of the bed and started to stand.

"No way in hell you're going in for this one," Matteo said. "But I was rather hoping you might be up for some triage."

"I'm fine," David snapped, struggling to his feet. Immediately his head started to spin, and he reached out for the bedpost to steady himself. Before he plunged back down onto his mattress, Solaina was at his side, steadying him.

"You can't go out there," she cried, pushing him back down into bed.

"We're short-staffed. Someone's got to—"

"I don't give a damn who does it," Matteo shouted from the hall, "as long as someone gets down there in two minutes."

"This is what we do here," David said, wincing as he went to stand up again. "Doesn't matter if we're up to it or not. We just do it because we're all they have."

"And it doesn't matter if the doctor keels over in the middle of it?" she asked, latching onto his arm as he wobbled to the door. "You're not up to this, and you know it. Matteo knows it."

"Thank you for caring about me," he said quietly. He slid his feet into a pair of deck shoes, without socks—too much effort to bend over to put them on—then leaned against the wall, trying to catch his breath. It wasn't like he was going to operate today. This was triage after all. He'd take the first look, make the assessments and assignments and move the patient along in the medical queue. He could do that from a chair, and with the way he was feeling, that might just be the case. "Remember when I told you my list of attributes…that I don't follow the rules, that I'm stubborn… I'm fine, Solaina, and with any luck this stubborn ass will be back in bed in an hour."

"It's difficult, taking care of a patient who doesn't want to be taken care of." She kissed him affectionately on the cheek.

"And it's difficult, being the patient when the nurse is so distracting." He returned her kiss, but to her lips. "I'm fine," he promised.

"Matter of opinion," she said, as he stepped out into the hall.

That much was true. He hurt like hell, and the dull headache that had been with him since he'd been attacked was sharpening. But he could do this. He had to. There was no one else. "There's a guest room across the hall. Settle in there for the night, and I'll stop by after I'm through in Triage and we can finish our talk."

"About my father and IMO?"

David nodded grimly as he lurched away, his left hand on the wall to keep him steady. "That, and other things." He would much rather talk about other things…things that lovers talked about. But they weren't lovers. He wasn't even sure if they were friends.

Solaina watched David grip the wall as he made his way to the reception area, and once he was out of sight she picked up the telephone next to his bed and made a collect call. It had been a year since she'd last talked with her father, and at the time she hadn't expected that it would be only a year until the next time. *"Bonjour, papa,"* she said when he answered, her voice so brittle it could have cracked and broken under the weight of a feather.

"Solaina, sweetheart. I've been expecting your call."

"I'll just bet you have," she said, already feeling the tension setting into her neck. She'd been the dutiful daughter for years, while her sister Solange had always rebelled. Somehow she'd thought being dutiful would earn love and respect. But Solange had been right about the whole thing. Bertrand Léandre wasn't about love or care or paternal concern. He was about blind obedience. It was his way, or he cut you off.

"So tell me about IMO, *papa.*"

"There's not so much to tell. They were in need of a good business director, and since you were involved with them in the loosest sense I thought it might be a chance for us to work together. Something to bring us back together. And it has."

"And you didn't tell me?"

"I knew that it would come up when the time was right. It's a worthy organization, Solaina. They needed someone with a name that would offer them more recognition than they were receiving."

Solaina shut her eyes. It always happened this way. He couldn't let go. Throughout her entire life, no matter where she went or what she did, her father always managed to impose himself in some fashion. He offered a financial contribution or a business consultation… No matter what, the minute he was in the door he took control. "Why?" she whispered.

"For you, darling. As always. I knew you were ending your job at the hospital."

Of course he had, even though she hadn't told him. He always knew.

"And I thought a position as the administrator of IMO might be a fine next step for you," he continued. "It would give you international prestige." He chuckled. "Take you into better circles where you might find the right man to father my grandson. It's time for that Léandre legacy to get under way. I'm not getting any younger, you know."

"This is about your legacy?" she sputtered. "You take over an organization with which I'm affiliated because you want a grandson?" Dear God, even from thousands of miles away he was all about control. It grew in him like yeast in rising bread dough.

"You keep yourself isolated, darling. I was just trying to draw you out a bit. For your own good, naturally."

Bertrand Léandre, an immense mountain of a man, chuckled on the other end of the phone line, and Solaina could just picture him. He was in his home in Miami at present. It was late there and he was sitting behind his large, nineteenth-century Moorish desk, smoking a Cuban cigar, mulling over his investment portfolio. He had a snifter of brandy in one hand, and he would glance over at the photo of her mother, Gabriella, as he took a sip. That was his custom, and if there was one thing she could count on with her father, he never changed his custom.

"What do you know about David Gentry?" she asked, trying to put off her anger. Going volatile on her father never accomplished anything, and since David believed IMO could be behind his attacks, which would make her father responsible, she had to know. Which meant she had to stay calm.

"Only that he's an idiot. Good doctor, but a terrible idealist. He left when the board revised policy. I wasn't there then, but that's what they've told me—and as far as I'm concerned, it was good riddance. Why?"

"Because someone's after him. They beat him within an inch of his life and I happened to be the one who stumbled on him and had to nurse him back to health." She wasn't about to mention David's hospital. Chances were her father already knew. But if he didn't she wouldn't be the one to tell him.

"You nursed him back to health?" Bertrand sputtered. "But I thought that after that nasty little Jacob Renner incident you'd given up all that and stuck to—"

"That nasty little Jacob Renner incident killed a man, *papa*." she snapped. "Do you remember? He died. They sued me and went after my license. And I did give up nursing after that. The kind that I really wanted to do."

"But they didn't win against you, and in the end you were much better off for it, getting away from all that patient care nonsense and into something more respectable. Something more in keeping with your credentials."

"In the end, Mrs Renner lost a husband, and her son a father." Because she hadn't recognized a simple symptom. And any future patients she might have had, if she'd made the switch to patient care, would have been better off for it. "So, are you after David Gentry, *papa?* Did you send someone after him for some reason?"

"You mean him and that little place he calls a hospital?"

So he did know. She wasn't surprised that he did. Neither was she surprised by the feeling of dread forming in the pit of her stomach. "Are you behind the vandalism here, and the attempt on his life?"

"And you think I would be?" He sounded more amused than outraged. A sound she knew, and one she hated. It was the one he always used when he was backed into a corner.

"I think you *could* be, but I hoped that you would not."

"David Gentry is not an issue with me. What's done with him is done. He put IMO in a bad spot publicly. His departure caused speculation and rumblings throughout the organization, and several of our financial backers have had a rethink on their contributions. A few have withdrawn and gone over to his clinic. Others have cut back to see how we're going to come out of this, which makes it very tough on the organization as a whole. And makes my position more difficult. But would I go after him because of all that?" That's where he stopped.

Solaina shut her eyes and shook her head. There certainly was no denial in that. But Bertrand Léandre would never admit his misdeeds. "Leave him alone, *papa*. If it's you, leave him alone."

"You're involved with him!" Bertrand accused. "You can do better than the likes of David Gentry, if that's what this is all about."

Her father would dictate her career *and* choose her husband. Now she remembered why she didn't get involved. Involvement meant control. And she'd had enough to last two lifetimes. "And you are more controlling than ever, *papa*. So listen to me, because I'm only going to say this once. I do not want— No, I demand that you stop interfering with David and his hospital. In any way, for any reason. Do you understand me?"

"You *want?* You *demand?* If you'd been a son, Solaina, I do believe you might have made me a proud man."

"Nothing in your life is worthy of pride, *papa*. Anything that might have been good died when *maman* did, and on that day I lost both parents—the one who always was, and the one who never was. If I'd have been your son, I would have hung my head in shame. As your daughter, even that much is not required of me."

"This is the thanks I get for all the trouble I've gone to, getting your name in the IMO arena for that head position?"

Solaina shut her eyes, torn between slamming down the phone and just plain ripping it out of the wall. "I don't want it," she snapped. "And I won't take it if it's offered."

"You took the last job."

"What?"

"The one in Chandella. You certainly don't think it just came out of the blue?"

"You influenced it?"

"I've influenced them all, Solaina. Every last one of them. And any job you want in the future is yours. All those grand offers you've had coming in… That's what a father's supposed to do, isn't it? Stand up for his child?"

"Silly me. And I though I'd earned them on my merits."

"Your merits are good, but merits with the Léandre name attached are better. And if you're considering something foolish, like staying at that hospital in Kantha, I'd suggest—"

"They need real nurses here, *papa*. Not the likes of me. You don't have to worry."

"But if your heart gets in the way…"

"I'm a Léandre. My heart *never* gets in the way."

As she hung up, Solaina looked at the phone for a moment, her mind more blank than anything else, then finally she remembered David. Had her father been able to hear love in her voice? Had she been so obvious, or had he merely been guessing?

"Merely guessing," she said hopefully, as she headed to the reception area to see how David was faring. It was too late to return to Chandella now anyway, and she might be of some use here tonight. Not much, but some, in spite of what her father thought of her.

CHAPTER NINE

"How often does this happen?" Solaina asked a young man who was carrying a small child in his arms. The little girl was three, maybe four years old. And she was too frightened to cry. Cuddled into the man's shirt, the occasional hiccup of a sob escaped her, but never a wail. "So many victims coming in at once. How often does this happen?"

"As far as mass casualties go, not as often as it used to. But incidents like this, where you have five or six people injured, it's pretty common. Are you a doctor?" he asked.

She shook her head. "Just a visitor." Solaina could see several cuts and scrapes on the little girl's arms. Nothing that looked serious, unless you were three or four, and scared to death. "What happened to her?" she asked.

"Collateral damage from some shrapnel. She caught a few pieces on her arms and legs. Nothing too bad, but the mine was a couple of decades old, and rusty, and she needs to be looked at, maybe have a tetanus shot, since it was out in a field."

David was busy attending a potential BK—below the knee—amputation, a rather messy job by a landmine. The patient was a young man, probably no more than twenty. He was sitting there quietly, hands folded in his lap, eyes cast downward as David went through the assessment.

She watched David work for a moment. He was compassionate. She could see more pain for the young man on David's face than the young man himself displayed. And David was efficient. As much pain as he was in himself, he was sorting out the particulars of the man's injury—the bleeding, the bone fragments, the options. He'd earned his reputation rightly, she decided.

In the next bed over from David, someone Solaina took to be a nurse was starting an IV in an older man. He was crying and moaning, rocking back and forth and holding onto his wrapped hand. David called out an order for morphine from across the way, to which the nurse quickly responded with a piggyback pouch of it to add to the IV drip.

"Can you take care of that?" David asked Solaina. "The little girl?"

"No!" she cried, instant panic setting in. "I don't do—"

"Yes, you do," he said. "And it's a simple thing, Solaina. Just a minor injury. You can take care of it, and I'm right here to help you if you need it! You're a good nurse."

"But, David…" Her protest vanished into thin air. David had gone back to concentrating on his patient and the man carrying the child was thrusting her into Solaina's arms.

"Her name is Pholla," he said. "Her father is on his way, once he gets clearance to cross the border." He whispered something to the child—Solaina assumed it to be in Cambodian—then handed her over. "I told her not to be afraid, that you would take good care of her." Without another word, the rescue worker turned and ran out of the door, leaving Solaina standing in the middle of the hall, holding a wounded child.

"I can do this," she said to Pholla. "It's just a few cuts, and I can really do this." The words were brave, but her hands were shaking because these were the same words she'd said to Jacob Renner all those years ago. *I can do this.*

Jacob's had been a simple case, really. Headache. Even the most inexperienced nurse could have handled that one. And when her night nurse in Emergency had called in sick, Solaina had had no reason to believe she couldn't do the job. No, she wasn't a critical care or emergency specialist. But she was certainly good enough for the minor things—the minor things like Pholla's shrapnel injuries. Like Jacob Renner's headache.

She looked at the little girl, and shuddered. "You're going to be just fine in a few minutes," she said, setting her gently on the emergency bed.

She had told the triage nurse, that night in Emergency when Jacob had come in, to send her only simple cases. The cuts, the bruises, the headaches. And that's exactly what she'd got. In the first hour she'd almost convinced herself that her time behind a desk hadn't diminished her skills as much as she'd believed, because the transition had been smooth. The patients came in, she treated them, they went home.

Then Jacob Renner had come in. He had been a nice man who'd had a tension headache. He'd had it all day, and it hadn't got better. Maybe he needed new glasses, he said. The ones he carried with him were thick, and Solaina certainly thought they might be the cause of his headache. Or maybe he'd eaten too much sugar. Sugar gave him migraines and his wife had baked cookies. So many causes, but when she told him he'd be fine, he believed her. So did his wife and ten-year-old son.

They believed and they trusted in someone who had gone

straight from nursing school into an administrative position, and had never passed by a patient on the way there. They trusted in someone whose practical skills were rusty.

But it never occurred to her that she couldn't do the job. And it never occurred to Jacob Renner's family that they would be going home without him that night.

The aneurysm in his brain burst before Solaina could get a doctor to look at him. She was handing him an ibuprofen tablet at the time. In retrospect, the doctors said he couldn't have been saved. He had been too far along and that even getting him to surgery to do the repair would have been futile because Jacob had been past the point of no return even before he'd got to the emergency department.

Solaina felt chilled, just thinking about it. It didn't matter what anybody said to make her feel better. A man had died because she hadn't been experienced enough to recognize his symptoms, and that had been the last night she'd ever treated a patient. Until David. And now Pholla. "Well, let's see what we can do to get you fixed up," she said to the girl, as she pulled on a pair of gloves.

"Need help?" David asked.

She glanced over at him and shook her head, gritting her teeth for the task ahead. "You look like the one who needs help," she replied as she helped Pholla get comfortable. David was pale, she noticed. And leaning a little too heavily against the bed. "You should be in bed yourself." Pulling back the blanket Pholla was wrapped in, Solaina saw much more than she was prepared for. Much more than the man who'd brought her in had disclosed. A few cuts, yes, but this child looked like she'd been tangled in barbed wire and had fought her way out. There were dozens of nicks on her legs—some deep, some not so deep. Some would need stitches, some just a good clean and one… Solaina took a good look at the cut on the back of Pholla's ankle. It was small, and not bleeding very badly. But its placement…right on the tendon. She took a better look, probed with her fingers and drew in a sharp breath. This was urgent! *The child was about to lose her foot!*

"Matteo," Solaina screamed, grabbing a roll of gauze bandage from a stand near the bed. Immediately she started wrapping the wound so the girl couldn't wiggle her foot and cause more damage. As Matteo came running, David hobbled around to that side of the bed to take a look.

"It can be saved," Solaina gasped, backing away as both men moved forward. "It's deep, but it's attached. The pedal pulse is weak, the foot is cold, sluggish reflexes and movement. But it can be saved, David. If she has surgery. *Now!*"

Then she turned and ran from the emergency room, fighting against the nausea threatening to overtake her. Slamming shut the door to the guest quarters, Solaina didn't even make it to the bed. Near the middle of the room she crumpled to her knees, then sat there, not crying, not thinking. Just numb. For how long? Long enough to let the incident with Jacob cycle through a dozen times, each precise moment of it playing out in her mind in vivid detail. First he was alive, then he was dead. Alive, dead. Alive… Dead…

She couldn't block it out. But she didn't want to. The reminder of what she'd done, always pounding away at her like it did, was the justified punishment that had kept her in her rightful place all these years. In the weak moments when she thought about returning to clinical practice, her perpetual punishment sealed that delusion away and beat the sure knowledge of where she did not belong right back into her.

"We all have traumas and bad experiences," David said a little while later, as he stepped into the room. His voice was so gentle it made her ache from wanting more of it. And ache even more, knowing she couldn't have it. What had just happened with Pholla had emphasized that—the way she'd panicked and run away. In a moment of weakness she'd thought she was up to it. David believed she was and she wanted desperately to trust that he was right. For him. But most of all, for her.

He was wrong, though.

"It's part of the medical existence," he continued. "You were outstanding in there, recognizing the severity of the laceration, making all the right assessments and getting it wrapped. She's going to be fine because of that."

Solaina didn't respond. There was nothing to say, because her trauma went far, far beyond a bad experience. She had killed someone after all.

"Do you want to talk about it?" he asked, struggling down to the floor next to her.

"There's nothing to say. I'm not a nurse. In training, yes. In practice, no. And expecting anything more of me is dangerous. You shouldn't have put me in that position, David. I took care of you out on the road because there was nobody else. But with Pholla there was. You have a hospital full of qualified staff and you shouldn't have…" She shook her head, swallowing back the lump in her throat.

"Panic attack?" he asked, taking hold of her hand.

Solaina nodded, but said nothing. There was nothing to say.

David scooted close to her, then put his arm around her shoulders. "Once, when I was a medical student, we had a young girl come in. She was probably five or six. Beaten by her stepfather. Beaten badly. She was assigned to me, so I did all the right tests—X-rays, lab work. I set her broken arm, bandaged her scrapes and turned her over to the authorities, who promised to take care of her. They said they would do the proper investigations, and I trusted that they would. Next week, same little girl, same stepfather. Irreparable brain damage. I quit being a doctor that day. Couldn't handle it, didn't want to handle it. Got a job in a car wash because I thought that would be a good place to figure out what came next in my life." He chuckled. "That lasted half a day. Want to know why?"

"Because you were a doctor," Solaina said stiffly.

"Because I was a doctor. Like you're a nurse. We all have those experiences that make or break us, Solaina. I don't know what happened to you, and I'm guessing you think yours broke you. But it didn't. You're still a nurse."

"An administrator of nurses," she corrected.

"A nurse," he insisted. "Or you wouldn't have stayed in the field. It's more than what you do. It's who you are."

"Who I am is someone who didn't recognize the symptoms of an aneurysm. I gave him ibuprofen for his headache and told him the doctor would be in to see him in a little while. A headache, David! His aneurysm burst while he was waiting, and he died, and that stupid ibuprofen didn't do him a bit of good because his nurse—the person he trusted to take care of him—couldn't take care of him. I didn't know enough. And you know what? I still have nightmares. And, yes, I do have panic attacks. My hands shake, I get sick to my stomach, my heart pounds, I go light-headed. All the time. They don't go away, and his face doesn't fade. And just now, when Pholla came in, I saw Jacob Renner. When I found you and had to take care of you, I saw Jacob Renner."

"But yet you don't give up, do you?"

"Nursing in the sense that I wanted to be a nurse…I never even had a start at it. When you come out of school with my credentials—a master's of science, a master's of business, a doctorate of nursing, they won't give you a bedpan. It's a desk, and a budget, and an administrative agenda."

"All those diplomas?"

"I was a professional student. Didn't want to face the real world, and I didn't for a long time. And the result was what is traditionally called an educated fool. By the time I got to nursing school and realized that was really what I wanted to do, I didn't stand a chance really. Except I didn't know that. And on the day I received my doctorate I was inundated with offers. So apart from my clinical practice as a student, I've had none. And I had no right going near a patient then. Or just now."

Solaina paused to draw in a deep, ragged breath, then she let it out slowly. "I'm sorry I made a scene in there, but you shouldn't have put me on the spot, David. I know my capabilities better than anyone else."

"And underestimate them," David said gently.

"My father has influenced every job I've ever had," she told him. "That's what he told me when I phoned him earlier. It seems like my career has never been mine, and I didn't even have the sense to know that. That car wash you were talking about—maybe I'll go get a job there for a while. See what I can figure out *for myself* this time, without anyone making the choices for me. Oh, and my father said he doesn't know anything about what's been going on at Vista."

Solaina scooted a little closer into David's embrace. It felt so good nice being there with him like that, better than it should have. And maybe this was all about her momentary collapse over her whole career situation and not at all about him. Somebody to cling to in a crisis.

But, then, maybe this was all about David.

"Do you want a job here, Solaina? Bad hours, lousy pay. The boss is pretty nice, though, I've heard." He tilted her face toward his. "Great benefits, when there's time."

Solaina's lips parted beneath David's as if that was natural thing between them, as if they'd been intimate lovers for ever and this moment was but one in some grander fate between them. One brief kiss had been what she'd promised herself at the start of it, but even before it began she was so hot for him she'd lost all control to pull back, or think, or even breathe normally. And when he ran his hand up her back, pulling her closer to him, she thrust her tongue into his mouth and kissed him hard, with all the pent-up emotions that now wanted to escape.

David's tongue met hers in the same sensation of heat and fury, and probed deeply, setting her entire body on fire. She wanted him here, and now, like she'd never wanted another man, and when he slid his hand under her shirt and cupped her breast, every little spark of resistence in her that might have surfaced was snuffed out. "David," she murmured, as his kisses trailed down her throat. "Yes…"

"Solaina," he moaned, fumbling, one-handed, to remove her shirt. It was a simple cotton pull-over, and such an obstacle for a man who had but one good arm to use.

"Your shoulder," she warned, eagerly helping him inch her shirt up over her head. "Are you sure you can—?"

"My shoulder's fine," he growled, reaching around to unfasten her bra even before her shirt was completely removed. With that he needed *no* help, and before she could draw in her next breath, her bra went sailing through the air and landed near the door.

"What about your patient?" she asked, as he skimmed his hand along her breast.

"In surgery," he said as he bent to take her nipple into his mouth.

"And Pholla?"

He teased her nipple with his tongue until it was standing erect, then he pulled away to admire his handiwork. "She's with Matteo. And it's just like I told you before. You are a nurse, Solaina. In every sense of the word. Even now, at the beginning of what should be one of the best nights of your life, you're thinking about your patients."

"One of the best nights of my life?" Gingerly, she began to pull his scrub top over his head. "You're setting your standards pretty high, aren't you?" she teased. He gasped as she struggled to get his shirt over his shoulder, so she slowed down a bit, even when all she wanted to do was rip it off him.

"I'll let you be the judge of that," he said, once the shirt was finally off and had been tossed on top of her bra.

"What about your ribs?" she asked.

"And what does my nurse prescribe?"

Instead of answering, Solaina pushed David gently back onto the floor, then took her place atop him, taking care not to press down against his chest. Then she looked down at him and smiled. "Does the doctor concur?" she asked, running her fingers lightly over the strain of his erection already pressing against his scrub pants.

"Concurs," he moaned, thrusting his pelvis up to meet her fingers, as he reached up to run his thumb over her erect nipples.

His hand lingered there only a moment, then he raised

himself up slightly, wrapped his hand around her neck and pulled her down to him, seeking her breast with his mouth…sucking and nibbling until she thought she was going to explode for wanting more of him…all of him. "Think we should turn off the lights?" he asked.

She had seen him naked already, as a patient. But now she wanted him naked, as a lover, wanted to look at him and admire him as a lover. "In the light," she said. Something about David drove her to be bold, and if this was the only time they were to be together, she wanted to remember every detail—of him, and of the best night of her life. And not in the dark.

David chuckled. "On the floor, in the light. You're not a conventional woman, Solaina Léandre."

"I don't have to be," she whispered, backing off him in order to remove his pants. "Not any more."

The scrubs tugged down easily, and so did his briefs, and for a moment Solaina simply admired him, all of him, as he watched her. "I've never been with a blond before," she said, almost shyly, as she stood to remove her own pants—baggy khaki cargos that slid down easily. Underneath, her panties were the sensible white cotton ones she wore for work, not one of the lacy pretties she kept tucked back in her drawer, barely worn. When she'd put on the whites this morning, she hadn't guessed she would be taking them off for David later on, and now she wished she were in the skimpy little blacks, or the satiny reds.

She knelt to straddle him again, then placed a light kiss on the flesh just below the bandages over his ribs. "So tell me. Do blonds have special needs?"

"The only special need this blond has is you, pretty lady. Did I ever tell you that you're the most beautiful woman I've ever seen?" he asked.

"In your delirium."

"I'm not delirious now, and you're still the most beautiful woman I've ever seen." He reached out to stoke her face. "I couldn't forget you, Solaina. I didn't know you, but all I could do was think about you. And the night your rescued me, it took me hours to realize it wasn't delirium."

"This scares me, David. I'm attracted to you…" She brushed her hand lightly over his abdomen, then smiled. "And I think you're feeling the same way…"

"Want me to show you just how much?" He grinned at her. "Because even with a chest full of broken ribs and a shoulder that's not working," he growled, grabbing her around the waist and pulling her down to him, "I still have a few tricks left." He ran his thumb over her lips, and followed it with a light kiss. "And parts of me are still in very good working order, if you'd care to find out."

Solaina pressed herself to him and heard his slight gasp, but she didn't pull back because his hand skimmed between them, seeking out that sensitive spot between her legs in a way that, once he found it, caused her to gasp. "Nice trick," she managed, as his fingers worked their magic, exploring the exquisite circle, until her breaths started coming in short, fast bursts as her body tried to explode in release.

But before it did entirely, David pulled away. "Condom," he groaned.

"I don't have one," Solaina moaned. It had been years since anything like this had come close to happening, and she wasn't on birth control. "Damn it," she muttered, partly from the physical letdown already sliding over her and partly from the emotional disappointment.

"In my shirt pocket."

"You were expecting this?" she asked, as she scrambled off him.

"I was praying for it."

His words made her throb. His touch, his smell, everything about David made her throb, and she was on the brink of needing him so badly that she would have forfeited the protection. She was glad he'd been prepared, and sad about it in a way, too. If this was to be their only night, which was probably the case as who knew where she'd be tomorrow, having all of him in the most intimate of ways would have been nice…wonderful.

This way, it was merely an encounter, but perhaps that was for the best. For the both of them.

"So, tell me how you like it, David." She straddled him again, then she slid her hand over his stomach—something she'd wanted to do the first time she'd seen him. "You've got a beautiful chest," she said, leaning carefully to press her breasts to him. "I noticed it the night I took off all your clothes."

"My chest? That's all you noticed?"

"I was being professional about it." She placed a light kiss on his belly, then moved down his right leg until she found his toes. "Your bruises look better," she said.

"Quit assessing the damage," he rasped, "and don't stop what you were doing."

She laughed. "But I thought you said I was a nurse."

"You're killing me, Solaina."

"I'm making this the best night you'll ever have, too." She retraced the trail up his other leg, then stopped at his belly and rose up enough to lower herself down onto him. "The very best night," she murmured, as she started to move up and down. If not for him, for her. Because this was no encounter, and David was not merely a casual fling on a hospital floor outside the little town of Kantha. She wasn't ready to admit love, or anything as profound as that. But if her life was any different, she might have. Love, or something like it. And she knew that after tonight nothing in her world would ever be the same.

"Ready?" she asked, fighting to restrain herself she wanted this so badly.

"Solaina," he moaned, and she knew it wasn't from pain. That was all it took. All notions of what ifs, and what might have beens were put aside for the urgency of *that* moment as she pressed herself exuberantly down on him, thrusting to feel as much of him in her as she could.

The feeling of him was almost more than she could endure as Solaina thrust herself even harder on David until she finally surrendered in a hard climax at the same moment he did.

There were no endearing moments afterwards, though. Not on a cold, hard floor under bright lights. The second Solaina rolled off David, he let out a moan that had nothing to do with ecstasy.

"I think I tore cartilage in my ribs," he gasped, grabbing himself across the chest and rolling over on his side.

Solaina sighed as she scrambled for their clothing. In one way they had both been correct—it *was* a night neither one of them would ever forget.

"It's probably just what you said," Matteo pronounced, looking at the fresh X-ray of David's ribs. "Torn cartilage." In the case of the human rib cage, cartilage connected rib to rib, and torn cartilage was simply when it tore away from the rib. It was painful, took a while to heal, and was usually not serious. "I'd diagnose bed rest, Davey, but I have a sneaking hunch that's how you got this injury."

"Shut up," David snapped, struggling to sit upright on the examining table. He wasn't angry about the torn cartilage. What he'd had with Solaina had been worth it. What he was angry about was finishing it with an injury—he'd wanted to talk for a while. Not pillow talk, as there had been no pillow involved in what they'd done. But he wanted to make sure that she was not feeling awful about her nursing skills again. He wanted to reassure her, and promise her, and say all the words it would take to make her understand that he'd seen her skill and it was good, and that she was being too harsh on herself.

And maybe, just maybe, there would have been an endearment or two in his words. Not in the permanent sense, as she was perfectly clear she didn't want that, but in the sense that he did care for her, and about her, and about what happened to her.

Of course, one rip of the rib and it had all been over.

"How are you going to work this out with Solaina?" Matteo asked straightforwardly.

"I don't know," David gasped, finally making it all the way up. "It's complicated. She has issues."

"And you don't?" Matteo laughed.

"Like I said, it's complicated."

"Foibles of youth, Davey. You played, obviously you played wrong, and you grew up. You're ready now."

"Maybe I am. But Solaina doesn't want involvement. She's told me over and over, in a dozen ways. And I honestly believe she'd go against her own feelings in this and walk away, she's so rock-ribbed about not getting involved. I don't know what to do about it either."

"So, like you said, it's complicated. But what's a little complication when there's true love in the balance? Right? Makes it better in the end when it finally works out."

True love? For him, yes. But for Solaina? He just didn't know. "Oh, and in case you're interested, Solaina had no idea her father was involved in IMO. She was shocked when I told her."

"You're sure of that?"

David nodded. It was about the only thing his poor body could still do without aching. "She called him and he claims he knows nothing about the attacks," David said, struggling to his feet. "Whether or not he's telling her the truth, I don't know. But Solaina is."

"She wouldn't lie to cover up for him?"

"Solaina is the most honest person I know. She wouldn't lie about anything." Two steps forward and he wobbled, then stopped. "I need a miracle cure, " he grumbled.

"You need a chariot." He pointed to one of the old-fashioned wooden wheelchairs sitting in the corner. High wooden back, hard wooden seat, it could be pushed only by an attendant, and it was none too comfortable for the passenger. But it was the only kind they had at Vista, something David was, all of a sudden, regretting.

"I can walk," he protested, shrugging off Matteo's attempts to help him walk across the examination room.

"Yeah, and if you run into the fair Solaina along the way, can you stand more torn cartilage, *or worse*?" He scrambled to the corner, then wheeled the chair up to the examining table for David. Gesturing for David to take a seat, Matteo grinned. "Until you're completely healed, I'm afraid I'm going to have to give you a rather severe restriction. Hate to do it, Davey, but you, of all people, should have realized what several broken ribs, combined with a beautiful woman, could lead to. Actually, in your case, *did* lead to."

"Yeah, yeah, I know," David grumbled, sitting down carefully. This time it felt like an entire army had stomped across his chest. Last time, when it had only been broken ribs…half an army. So Matteo didn't have to warn him because, like it or not, he had the hospital to consider first. And what he'd just done could have compromised care at the hospital if he wasn't determined to work through the pain, which he was. Grit his teeth and see the patients. That was his responsibility, that's what he would do. What he *had* to do.

Still, as Matteo wheeled him back to his room, a slight smile crossed David's lips. The pain would go away eventually. The memories wouldn't. In the end, what he'd had with Solaina had been worth the inconvenience. Anything with Solaina, he was beginning to realize, was worth the inconvenience.

Solaina stayed in the shower until the warm water started to chill, then she stepped out, dried herself and tugged on some fresh surgical scrubs. Looking down at herself, she wondered why she still pretended. In the emergency area a little while ago, with the child Pholla, she'd proved she was anything but a nurse, running out the way she had. So maybe it was over— the whole nursing phase of her life. Her job in Chandella would end soon, and the hiring pool was contaminated, so to speak. *Thanks to her father.* Maybe it was time to face facts and start in a new direction.

"Like what?" she snapped, sliding into bed.

David had asked her to stay, and as appealing as that was, it was also a disaster—or at least, it would turn into a disaster for him once he got over his infatuation and realized that she wasn't what he insisted she was. It would cause problems between them—his refusal to accept her as she was, her inability to be the nurse he expected. And personal and professional things did get tangled. She'd lived that life with her parents. There were few separations—her mother had been a doctor. That's who she'd been, professionally and personally. It's what had shaped her life, rooted her opinions, dictated her attitudes. No separations in all the facets of Gabriella Bontecou Léandre. The doctor and the woman had been one and the same. In David, the doctor and the man were one and the same, too. What he did was who he was, and it ran deep in him.

For her to stay would disappoint him on the professional level. Eventually that would seep into the personal. And she couldn't bear that to happen, no matter how she felt about him. David deserved much more than what she could be for him.

Tonight, they'd made love instead of resolving things. But what about next time, when he forced her into a medical situation she didn't want to be in, then expected her to perform? And the time after that?

It would happen again. She was sure of it.

Snuggling in under the sheets, Solaina stared up at the dark ceiling. "I can't believe you did that," she whispered to herself, resisting the urge to run her hands over her lips…her shoulders…her breasts…all the places he had kissed. Making love…*and it had been making love*…in the middle of the floor with a man she'd known but a few days. But she was falling in love with him, for so many reasons she didn't understand, even though she'd put away the notion of that ever happening to her.

Somehow, her father always got in the middle of her life—dominating, controlling, always expecting something.

Oh, she could stay in Kantha, as she was about to become a woman without an aim in life. But deep down in the recesses of her heart, she knew that wouldn't work. Tonight she'd taken care of that little girl because David had insisted. He believed in her, and she loved him for that. But that belief came from love and not logic, and he simply didn't understand that telling her she was a good nurse did not make it so. He was looking at her through the eyes of love and it was a wonderful fantasy, but it wasn't enough.

Staying in Kantha with him wouldn't make it so either. "So I'll leave," she whispered. In the clear light of day she would walk away and never look back. Because if she did look back and caught even the slightest glimpse of everything she wanted and couldn't have, she would end up doing something she would regret. Or they both would come to regret.

Jacob Renner… His face floated over her as she drifted off to sleep.

CHAPTER TEN

"Solaina?" David whispered, sitting down on the bed next to her.

She'd heard him come in, and pretended to sleep. Right now she simply couldn't face him. He would kiss her again, or ask her to stay, and all her resolve of just an hour ago would fly right out the window, leaving her to gather it back once he left again. So she ignored him.

"Solaina," he whispered again, this time laying a gentle hand on her shoulder. "We need to talk."

There were no more words. What he expected of her she couldn't be. That's all there was.

"Look, I can't even pretend to understand what you're going through with your father, with your memories of Jacob Renner, with your career…"

"Do you believe my father's the one behind the accidents?" she said, her face still to the wall.

"Honestly, I don't know. IMO wasn't happy when I left. It put them in a bind…"

She finally rolled over, but only to her back and not to face him. "He wanted me to take over the administrative operations for IMO. That's why he took a seat on the board.

His choice for me, David. He saw me as the administrator, and he was arranging it because that's what he thought I should be."

"You'd be very good at it," David said.

"But that's not the point. It wasn't my choice. Just like taking care of Pholla wasn't my choice. I've had a lifetime of people making decisions for me, telling me who I am and what I can do. My father has paved the way for me even when I didn't know it. And you forced me into treating that child, David."

"Because you're a good nurse, Solaina. Even if you don't see it. You had a incident with one patient, but you shouldn't let that influence your entire career." David pulled back the sheet, pulled up her scrub top and placed a kiss to her belly button. Then he straightened back up and struggled to grab a breath. "Matteo might have been right about his diagnosis," he groaned, wrapping his arms around his midsection.

"Bed rest, alone?"

"Something like that."

"Serves you right," she said, climbing out of bed. She was glad of the distraction, because David simply didn't understand. He saw what he wanted to see. And he loved the perception of her. That was probably the saddest thing of all, because she could have been all that at one time. And she desperately wanted to be what he saw now. "Serves you right for disobeying doctor's orders," she said, trying to keep the sadness out of her voice. It had been her choice after all. When it was all said and done, it had always been her choice.

Once Solaina's bare feet hit the floor, David toppled into the spot where she'd been lying. "Now what are you doing?" she asked. As if she didn't know. He intended to stay there.

That was obvious in the way he was already settling in, and she wanted him to stay. One more night… "Getting ready to tear the rest of the cartilage away from your ribs?"

"Believe me, the thought has crossed my mind. But right now I'm afraid I'm only half the man I was on the floor, and the half crawling into your bed intends only to sleep. *With you,* I hope. We did it once, and it was rather pleasant."

"You accused me of snoring," she said. He was so hard to resist. If she were smart, she'd be on her way back to Chandella right now, instead of tempting herself to sleep with him. If she had any sense, she'd find another room and lock the door before he got there. If she had any willpower when it came to David, she wouldn't be inching her way back to the bed. Which she was. Rather quickly, at that.

"Snoring in a sexy way, though," he added, grinning.

"You called it a chainsaw."

"But a very sexy chainsaw." He stretched out next to the wall and patted the empty space beside him.

"You know we shouldn't be doing this. It's not going anywhere, David." Truer words had never been spoken. Even so, those eyes…that devilish smile… And, oh, how she was growing to love his blond hair… Such an enticement, and she desperately wanted to be enticed. "What we have, what we did…that's just—"

"You talk too much," he interrupted. "Out here, in my world, we take things one step at a time. That's the only way we can get through. One step at a time, Solaina." He patted the bed again, grinning. "One snore at a time."

"I don't snore," she grumbled, climbing in next to him and snuggling into his side. Gingerly, of course, since he was all aches and pains. Even her slight movement on the bed evoked an involuntary wince from him. "And I won't do anything to rip any more cartilage."

"Maybe a kiss?"

"Where?" she asked.

"Where it doesn't hurt." He pointed to his left elbow and Solaina kissed it lightly. Then he pointed to his left shoulder and Solaina raised herself up and placed a kiss there. Then his throat and jaw. As she reached his earlobe, David exhaled a long, deep sigh and she knew he was asleep.

Smiling, she shut her eyes and decided to drift off with him. One day at a time. Maybe he was right. Maybe in one more day she would have an answer. "One day," she murmured as sleep began to claim her.

"I love you, pretty lady," David whispered back.

Had he really said that, or was it a dream? She wasn't sure, and maybe it was better that way.

Still, they were such nice words to take with her into her sleep.

One more minute, she kept telling herself. *That's all I want. Just one more minute, then I'll leave while he's still sleeping.* But by the time the next minute came along, she was already promising herself yet another minute. *Just one more minute.*

It was so difficult even thinking about leaving him…and it wasn't quite dawn when Solaina shut her eyes for the tenth time since she'd crawled in next to David. *One more hour,* she promised herself, and this time she meant it. One more hour and she would begin that long road back to Chandella. With this promise, though, her eyes were not shut for more than a few seconds when she heard thunderous steps in the hallway outside her door and a frantic cry from someone banging on David's door across the hall. "The hospital's on fire," the female voice was screaming. "Dr Gentry, the hospital is on fire!"

It took a second for Solaina to fully comprehended the words, and she bolted up out of bed. David woke up and struggled to sit up.

"Fire," she gasped. "The hospital's on fire. We've got to get out!"

He was trying to push himself over to the edge of the bed, and going about it so slowly she realized that was all he had in him. She grabbed David's arm and pulled at him, not even bothering to protect his injuries, until he was on his feet. Then she scrambled to grab his shoes.

"Take these," she said, shoving them into his hands, "and get out of here. Right now. Go outside, take a count of everybody who comes out. And make sure they stay as far away from the building as possible. Get names, David," she continued, thrusting her overnight bag at him. "I have a notebook in there. Write down the name of every patient who comes out and tag it on them. And triage them, if they're injured. I'm also going to try and get the patient charts out to you, so you can compare—see if anybody's been left behind."

She ran to the door, then turned back to make sure David was behind her. "I'm going to go help evacuate the patients. You take care of yourself, because I do love you, David. I want you to know that in case—"

"No," he choked.

"This is something I can do, David. Something I'm trained to do." She reached to brush his cheek, then disappeared into the crowd in the hallway, trying to make it to the exit.

"Where's Davey?" Matteo yelled at her.

"On his way outside to do triage. How many patients do we have to evacuate?"

"Twenty who aren't ambulatory at all, another ten who are ambulatory with assistance, and twenty-five who can manage on their own."

"Staff?"

"Most of them live in the outbuildings. We have eight live-in staff and I assume they're helping, but I—"

"Look," Solaina said, stopping him, "you stay with the non-ambulatories. Get them out to David. Now! I'll go make sure everybody else is getting out."

"Fire's in the surgery," he shouted, heading out the door. "It's at the opposite end to the patient wards, and it's contained right now, as far as I can tell. But be careful, Solaina. Davey will kill me if the lady he loves doesn't come through this."

The lady he loves… The words played through her mind, over and over, as she ran down the hall to the ambulatory ward, passing, on her way, several of the medical staff who were assisting patients to safety. Solaina grabbed one young nurse, who looked more baffled than useful. "Get all the patient charts that you can," she yelled over the clamor and cries of those fleeing the building. "Don't put yourself at risk, but try to find as many as you can, then get them out to Dr Gentry."

"But I need to—"

"No, you *need* to get all the patient charts," Solaina shouted. "Before the fire spreads and we can't get to them. Find someone to help, if you have to." She spied an older man, a patient, shuffling down the hall. He didn't appear at all bothered by the frenzy going on around him. "Do you speak English?" she called to him.

"OK," he responded, giving her a hesitant smile. "Speak English some."

"Can you help us?"

"I can help you OK," he responded again.

"Take him," Solaina told the nurse. "Throw the charts from the first unit on a cart and have him wheel them outside, then keep doing that until they're all safe. Do you understand?"

Both the nurse and the man nodded, even though Solaina was sure the man didn't understand, then they headed off together in the direction of the nursing station outside the patient ward closest to the fire. The ward most likely to burn down first.

"And you…" Solaina shouted at another attendant. "Go to the emergency area and take as many supplies out as you can. Oxygen and masks, blankets—anything. Grab some of the ambulatory patients to help you, if you need it."

The young man nodded, then ran in the opposite direction to Solaina toward Emergency. She stood there for a moment, making assessments. The fire was still contained, the smoke under control, but it might only be a matter of minutes before the fire spread to something combustible, like some of the medical gases. Thank God the surgery was so far away from the patient wards. That was the only saving grace in all this. The patients would all escape and, with luck, much of the necessary equipment could be dragged out before the full fiery force claimed the hospital.

By the time Solaina reached the ambulatory ward, it was practically deserted. A few stragglers had hung back, trying to gather the scattered belongs they had brought to the hospital with them—probably the only things they had left, she thought briefly. "Can anyone here speak English?" she shouted.

One of the older men yelled, "I can."

"Then tell everybody I need their help. As they can walk, I want them to help those who can't walk to get to safety outside." One little old woman in a curtained-off area was fighting frantically to pull her meager possessions into the bed sheet, and it broke Solaina's heart to have to tell her, and all these people, that the belongings couldn't go, not as long as there were lives to save. "We need everybody who is able to help. And those who are not able can gather up all the belongings left behind and carry them outside. If they're ready to go right now! Because we have to get out."

She could feel the heat starting to rise, feel the sweat from it starting to saturate her clothing, smell the cloying odor of smoke sticking to her skin. The medical gases in the surgery—was there enough time to secure the hospital before they exploded? Before the entire building caught fire?

"Tell them to hurry," she instructed the man, who translated her words. "And if they see *any* flames or smoke, to get out immediately." In a flash, six people dropped their lifelong possessions to the floor and ran to her. Even the little old lady who was wresting her treasures into the sheet willingly left it all behind to follow Solaina out into the hall.

No one stayed behind to retrieve anything. Brave, gallant people, she thought. People who didn't deserve the fate that had brought them here, and who didn't deserve this fate now. No wonder David loved this life. The people here made the sacrifices worth everything.

The people here, so many now starting over. Dear God, she knew what she had to do if she got out of here alive. Suddenly, it was all very clear.

In the hall, just down the corridor, Solaina and her group

were greeted by a small army of people on crutches, and even a few people who were crawling, all on their way out. Just beyond them the smoke was getting thicker near the entrance to the non-ambulatory wing—the wing where nobody walked, crawled or even hobbled on crutches. These people in front of her would make it out. They would be slow, but they would find safety, so she motioned for her little group of rescuers to pass them by, and they continued down the hall until they came to the ward with the biggest need. The totally helpless. The bed-bound. There were still a half dozen of them to be rescued, she discovered as she ran through the door.

The staff was making a gallant effort at rescue, carrying one patient at a time or pushing them on any trolleys available. But it was slow going, and as she looked at the faces of those still there, she noticed a certain calmness, and thought of her smiling, red-lipped Buddha who had that same calmness. These people were simply awaiting their destiny—to be rescued, or die.

It was so smoky in there that Solaina wished she had thought to find masks. The oxygen was being sucked out by the smoke and the heat was far worse in that ward than in any other area she'd seen so far. But they were close to the surgery and time was running out! "Get them out any way you can," Solaina shouted. Not that she needed to. Her band of rescuers was already doing just that—throwing themself into the full effort, shoulder to shoulder, with the majority of the medical staff.

It took mere seconds to load the remainder of the non-walking patients into wheelchairs and onto stretchers, and even Solaina was amazed by how quickly the ward was evacuated. Seemingly in the blink of an eye it was empty. She was the only one left, and it was eerie, standing there alone for that fraction of a second, because she would be the last person here. *The last person ever.* In another few minutes this ward would be gone. Then, in another few minutes after that, David's whole hospital.

"Where else, Matteo?" she shouted, as he ran by the door, pushing a cart with two grown men clinging together on top of it. "Where else would I find people in this hospital?"

"Just the wards," he shouted back. "And they're empty. There's no one in Surgery or Emergency. And the staff is all out and accounted for. Davey's made sure of that. Now, you get yourself out of here, Solaina. We've done all we can do."

Not very far away she heard the first explosion, and felt the rumble of it down the hall and into the ward. The impact slammed her into the wall. "Dear God," she whispered, the full force of what was happening finally hitting her. Somebody had done this to David—to his hospital. The same person who had almost killed him. Her father?

She wanted to crumple to the floor, to her knees, and cry for David, but a second explosion followed almost immediately after the first, and Solaina took one final look around the ward to check for anyone who might have been left behind. Fear caused strange reactions in fires. It made people hide in the worst possible places—under beds, in closets, behind cabinets. She'd learned that in the numerous emergency training sessions she'd taken over the years, and now, as she swept back through the ward, looking under beds and behind curtains and closets, she was relieved to find the room totally vacated.

"Get out!" someone screamed at her from the hall. "The fire's spread out of the surgery."

When she heard that, she glanced first at the ceiling, then

at the wall. There was still a little time, she knew. Even though the smoke was beginning to roll in, she still had time to get back to another ward for one last check.

On her way out of the door into the hall, Solaina grabbed a towel off the end of one of the patient beds, poured water on it from a basin and clamped it over her mouth and nose. Then she ran as hard and fast as she ever had in her life to the next ward and made a quick check. Empty, thank God.

She was still well ahead of the fire, she thought as she ran into the hall. At the far end, the non-ambulatory ward from which she'd just come moments earlier, she could see a blaze engulfing the wooden door and spreading its way over the wooden walls in the hall. Meaning she had only seconds to get out of there now that the fire was spreading. The building was constructed of wood—probably bamboo. The fire was greedy now, and it would devour the entire structure withing minutes.

But the last ward! Ambulatory. She'd been there already, seen everyone leave. No time to go back for one last check. It was time to get herself out of the hospital and let the fire finish its vile job.

Halfway to the door, Solaina heard someone shouting. "Davey says Pholla is missing." She knew Matteo's voice, but couldn't see him through the smoke. Her eyes were streaming now, and breathing through the wet towels was becoming more and more difficult. And the heat… Dear God, she was so hot her skin felt scorched. Maybe it was.

"Solaina," he shouted, "where are you?"

"Which ward?" she screamed, praying it was ambulatory, because it was the only one ahead of her and now there was no way back. The fire was fully in control in the other wards and fighting its way to get through to this one.

* * *

"Over here. Bring him over here!" David shouted above the moans and wails of the patients. "And get blankets on those people over there." He pointed to a group of three older women stretched out on the ground. They were only a couple of days post-surgery—one with an above the knee amputation, one with serious shrapnel wounds in both legs and one who'd lost a couple of fingers. If he didn't find a way to get them into shelter fast, they could die of shock or other complications. "Then get them into one of the staff's living quarters and make sure someone is with them at all times." Their various conditions alone didn't make them critical, but their conditions combined with their age did.

He made his way over to a man lying on top of a cart. The only light came from the fire, but David didn't need much light to see the man's difficulties. He was gasping for breath, probably from panic—and who couldn't blame him? If there was time, David would have been feeling the same way. He spoke a few words to reassure the man, even though he spoke no English, then took hold of his wrist to assess his pulse. "It's good," he said, tucking the man's arm back under the blanket. "OK." He gave him the international thumbs-up sign, and the man returned it.

The man pointed to David's bandages, and it was the first time David actually noticed that he hadn't bothered pulling on a shirt. "OK?" the man asked, genuinely concerned.

David nodded, even though he was not OK. Not while Solaina was still inside and he couldn't do a thing to help her.

He glanced at the hospital and sucked in a sharp breath. Solaina and the child. They would be OK, too. They had to be. "OK," he whispered, moving on to the next patient, a young woman with a leg reconstruction. He'd done the surgery himself, just over a week ago, and she was coming along splendidly now. She was on the ground, and as David bent to down examine her the pinch of his ribs sucked the breath right out of him. It took several seconds before he was able to draw in another breath, and it was ragged. He'd just done himself more damage. Ripped more cartilage.

Biting his lower lip against the pain, he steadied himself in a squatting position and pulled back the woman's blanket to take a look at her bandages. "Sok," he said, "how are you doing?"

"Fine, Doctor," she said in fluent English. "Don't worry about me. I'm fine."

He glanced back at the hospital again, struggled for another breath, then let it out slowly. "We'll have somebody get you into one of the other buildings in a little while," he said, even though, unlike Sok, nothing at all was fine with him. And it had nothing to do with the pain tearing his body to pieces and everything to do with the pain tearing his heart apart.

"Get out of there, Solaina," he prayed aloud.

"She should be in ambulatory," Matteo yelled.

"I'm right there so I'll go get her—you get out of here and help David!" Solaina sputtered, not sure if her voice was strong enough to carry now that her lungs were beginning to fill with smoke. Thirty seconds, she told herself. *That's all I have.* More of that training coming into play. A requirement of her job—to anticipate and direct all emergencies. Fire included. For administrators only. "Pholla," she cried, bursting through the doors of the ambulatory ward. "Pholla, where are you?"

The ward was smoky, but not as bad as the hallway. Still, her eyes were streaming even more now and she was forced to squint. "Pholla?" she called, then started to cough. Twenty-five seconds…twenty-four…

"Pholla, please, come out, sweetie." Twenty-three…twenty-two…

"Come on, Pholla. I want to take you outside." Twenty-one…twenty… "Where you can breathe."

Solaina looked under the beds as best she could, first up one side of the ward then down the other, then she shoved aside a supply cabinet sitting against the wall near the middle of the room. No sign of Pholla anywhere. Twelve…eleven… Her lungs were finally giving out, trying to seize up on her. Time was running out now—for the little girl, for her. "Pholla," she cried, determined not to give up, then she doubled over in a gut-wrenching cough. "Sweetie…" she forced out.

Nothing. And now the smoke was so thick she could barely see her hand in front of her face.

She looked up at a window just above her head—so much fresh air just on the other side. But if she broke it, the draft might suck the fire right in… No other choice. She had to get out of there. Now! *But if she's still in here somewhere…* Three…two…one. Time was up. To survive, Solaina had to abandon her search. Run for her own life. *Get out of there, Solaina!*

Was that David calling her?

"Pholla," she called one last time.

Get out of there, Solaina!

The sick feeling of abandoning the child was more unbearable than the heat and the smoke and the lack of oxygen, but before Solaina gave herself over to total defeat she ran to the middle of the room, shut her eyes and visualized what she had seen the first time she'd come in the ward only minutes ago, when she'd been evacuating the other patients. The beds, the cabinet… Had that been all? *Think!* The beds, the cabinet…the laundry basket! In the corner to the right of the door.

"Pholla!" she screamed, running straight there. It was too smoky to have a good look inside, so she thrust her hands into the laundry—and there she was. Pholla! Nestled among the dirty sheets and towels. Her foot was bandaged from the surgery, and she was clinging to a rag doll.

Solaina sucked in a breath and held it as her fingers sought the pulse in Pholla's neck.

Still alive! Mercifully, thank her smiling Buddha, the little girl was still alive.

Solaina scooped her up, cradled her to her chest and crashed through the door into the hall, stopping only for a fraction of a second to get her bearings in the gray haze now swallowing every inch of available air. Once she'd fixed her position, and remembered which way the door was, she ran straight outside, then collapsed on the ground, several steps away, still clutching Pholla to her chest.

And breathed!

By the time Matteo and another of the hospital workers pulled them away, the fire was raging throughout the hospital. Nothing and no one in there now could have been saved.

"Solaina," David said, holding the oxygen mask over her face. God, how he wanted to hold her in his arms. He should have been the one in there, leading the patients to safety, organizing their escape, saving Pholla. Not Solaina!

"I'm fine," she gasped, pushing away her oxygen mask. "How's Pholla?"

"No worse for wear. Poor little thing's been through a hell

of a lot today, but she's fine. Breathing on her own. Scared to death."

"Are they going to save anything?"

David looked at the building. The fire brigade from Kantha had arrived, but they carried buckets, not hoses. And they were running back and forth from an outside pump, transporting one bucket of water at a time. It was a futile effort, he knew. The flames licked at the wooden structure as greedily as a hungry child licked an ice-cream cone.

"No," he said. "Nothing."

"David, I'm so sorry…" she choked.

"No one died, Solaina," he said. "And except for some smoke inhalation, everyone's fine. That's all that matters." Everything—every hope, every dream—had been engulfed in that orange glow, but in the moments when he'd thought Solaina and Pholla might not make it out of there, he'd realized how much Solaina had become such a big part of those hopes and dreams. And the possibility of losing her… He swiped at the tears still streaming down his face. "That's all that matters," he whispered.

For the next several minutes no one said a word. Not Solaina. Not David. Clinging together so tight they almost drew the same breath, they simply watched as the volunteers threw themselves into dousing the fire, almost mesmerized by the steady rhythm of the effort. Several people filled the buckets while others carried them to the men who had now grabbed shovels and were throwing dirt, as well as water, on the inferno. It was a slow process, though, and one meant only—now—to stop the fire spreading to the other buildings. There was no longer any hope for the hospital. Everyone knew that, and the despondency of fighting a lost cause was already showing in the weary slump of shoulders and the sad expressions.

The fire was simply overtaking the hospital faster than they could put it out, and patches of brush between the hospital and the nearest outbuilding had also gone up in flames.

"They don't see it," Solaina said, pointing to the fire that had jumped the break. "What's in there?"

"Medical supplies—things needed for rehabilitation. The things we send home with our patients, like wheelchairs and crutches. And we store some of their personal belongings in there, too."

"I can save it," Solaina cried, jumping up.

"No!" he yelled. David went to grab her hand, but she pulled away from him. "Solaina, stop!"

Too late. She was off toward the jump fire before he could get himself off the ground. "Damn it," he muttered, following her and quickly finding out that he simply could not run. "Solaina," he screamed. "It doesn't matter! Those things don't matter!"

Solaina didn't listen to him, though. Instead, she grabbed a shovel brought in by one of the Kantha volunteers and began to beat at the tiny trail of brush fires, trying to hammer them into the earth. He could see her in the distance, alternately shoveling the dirt then pounding then shoveling.

By the time he reached her, several volunteers had joined her and the fire was stopped short of the storage building. "Solaina," David snapped, grabbing her arm and holding on for dear life because he was afraid she would run off to fight yet another battle. "What the hell were you thinking, running after the fire like that?"

"I was thinking of their personal posessions, and how much

they've already lost. And I was thinking of the wheelchairs and crutches they would need, even though the hospital is gone, and how long it might take to replace them, and what their lives might be like without them." She took in a deep breath, then coughed. "And I was thinking that I wasn't going to let my father destroy everything."

"Your father?"

"My father. He did this, David. You think that, don't you?" She swatted angrily at a large piece of ash floating down from the sky.

He didn't know what to say. It could have been an accident. Or of Bertrand Léandre's doing. That was Matteo's theory anyway, though David wasn't so sure.

Most likely the cause wouldn't be determined, because out here forensics wasn't sophisticated. Unless someone had actually left behind a gas can, or claimed responsibility, it would go down as an accident. "Solaina, I don't know. And even if he did do this, it's not your fault. And it doesn't matter what's happened now. Everybody's safe, and we can rebuild."

"I'm so sorry," she cried, then coughed again. This time David pulled her to his chest.

"I know you are, pretty lady. But you had nothing to do with this, no matter how it started. Trust me, Solaina. This is not your fault." And if he had to say those exact words to her every day for the rest of his life, he would. Tonight, when he'd thought he might lose her, he'd realized that if she came out of the burning building, he would never, ever let her go. He couldn't. Whatever it took…

But now wasn't the time to say such things to her. She had

too many wounds that needed healing first. "I need your help, Solaina. I can't do this alone." This time around, he couldn't.

Several of the locals, not involved in fighting the fire, had appeared at the hospital by the time the fire was extinguished. Women with children, older people. Then tables appeared from nowhere, set up with pitchers of water and fruit juices. And there, before the break of day, in a remote jungle hospital, everyone worked together cohesively, as if they came together often to fight a fire. No one told these people what to do. No one even asked them to do it. But they did, willingly, and it was unlike anything Solaina had ever seen. These wonderful people again...

She accepted a cup of water from an old woman, then held it up for David to drink as the two of them still clung together in the shadows, watching the hospital finally collapse in on itself. It was surreal, and in a way anticlimactic. Half an hour ago it had been there, now it wasn't. And it was time for her to do what she did best. "I'm going to start separating the patients by their needs," she said. "Some need immediate shelter, and we'll have to make arrangements to get them to the hospital in Chandella right away."

It was hours away, so in the meantime she would have the volunteers clear out all the outbuildings and make the staff quarters ready. Any shelter was better than none. "I'll call them and see what they can send in the way of transport. And maybe the people who don't need real hospitalization can go home with some of the people who live in Kantha. I'll get one of your staff members to ask around."

"You're a good nurse, Solaina Léandre," David said.

"A good administrator," she replied.

"A good administrator, too. But also a good nurse. And before you start arguing, I'm going to go start a round of medical assessments while I still have a little strength left in me. We've got patients in all kinds of conditions out here, and even with one arm I'm still a doctor."

"You should rest and let Matteo and some of the others take over."

"Is that the administrator or the nurse speaking?"

"It's the woman who cares about you speaking."

"Then the woman who cares about me knows what I have to do, doesn't she?"

Solaina nodded. But would the man who cared about *her* understand what *she* had to do? She reached up and brushed his lips with a quick kiss. "You take care of yourself, David. No matter what, you take care of yourself."

CHAPTER ELEVEN

VICTORIA BRUMLEY always set a nice spread. That's one thing Solaina could count on when she dined with her neighbors—everything done properly. And tonight Victoria had outdone herself. The cuisine was French, starting with a very proper *soupe de piments d'espelettes* and following though to the luscious *crêpes aux poires*. All very nice, served on Victoria's finest china. But Solaina barely touched it. She'd eaten enough to make a polite pretense, but that was all. That's all she'd eaten for weeks now.

"He's going to rebuild," Howard said, pouring himself a third glass of wine. "And I know he'd like you to be there. He hasn't changed his mind on that. He's still quite daft about you, you know."

"My new job is fine," Solaina replied. Actually, she liked her new position. It was as a volunteer in a little clinic outside Chandella. She worked with children mostly. Giving shots, taking temperatures, passing out lollipops. And, yes, bedpans. This was nursing at its roots, and a very good place for her. A place to heal, and to learn. A place to move on from Jacob Renner. Her start.

"Well, I think all that rebuilding is nonsense," Victoria

said, pulling the wine bottle away from Howard. "It will take months, and I think David would be better off with his career if he returned to Toronto."

Solaina cast her a curious glance. In all the time she'd known Victoria, this was the first time she'd heard the woman offer an opinion about medicine. Normally she deferred in that topic to her husband, and talked about travel and cuisine and going to the opera in Italy, or some such. "David needs his career here," Solaina said. "It's where his passion is." A passion she was just beginning to understand.

"If it was only about his career, that would be fine." Victoria rose from the table and floated across the room to the buffet to fetch the silver coffee server. "But he involves so many other people. And look at *you*, Solaina. It's been four months now, and you're still in a bad way over him."

"She's in love with him," Howard supplied. "That's why she's in a bad way. Because she blames herself for his ruin. Which entitles her to be in a bad way."

"His ruin maybe, but her salvation in the long run."

Solaina looked back and forth at the couple as they squabbled over her. It wasn't a side of them she'd seen before, and she wondered if she should merely take her leave before their squabble escalated into a battle.

"And what do you mean by that?" Howard stormed.

"You know what I mean by that. All these years, Howard, and all the time I've been alone while you were off chasing after one cause or another. I didn't mind for a while, because I admired what you did. Admired your work. And I was proud of it. But somewhere in those years I grew old. Old, and alone. And I've never been to the opera in Italy, Howard. There was always something else in the way."

Victoria carried the coffee service to the table, but Solaina declined, so the older woman merely took her place at the end of the table opposite her husband. Looking sad, Solaina thought. She did look sad, and lonely. When the wide-brimmed hats were off, underneath Victoria was a sad, aging woman. And a bitter one, Solaina could tell, from the flash in her eyes.

"But I always thought we would have our retirement," Victoria said, the momentary fight draining out of her voice. "I counted on our retirement, Howard. Then it would be just the two of us. Nothing and no one else. Just us." She drew in a frail, shuddering breath. "But I was wrong, of course. You found IMO. And I abided by that. Then you left, and I thought it was finally my turn. But you went to help start David's hospital." Victoria sat her cup on the table and glared across at her husband. "It took you all of one week out of IMO to start up Vista with David. And leave me alone again, naturally." She looked over at Solaina, her eyes softening. "You see, this way it's so much better for you, dear. No bother over a husband who is never there. You deserve a better life than that."

"A better life!" Howard yelled.

It was the first time Solaina had ever seen his composure break, and she scooted away from the table, ready to make her exit and leave the Brumleys to work out their difficulties in privacy.

"A better life," Victoria shouted back. "You gave me things, Howard. *Things.* Look around." She stood up and spread her arms in a wide, sweeping gesture, the silk sleeves of her caftan floating like paper kites on a gentle March breeze. "Look around. That's all this is. *Things.* And that's what I've had from you all these years. But I stayed, because I always did count on having time together or I wouldn't ever have…"

She stopped short, then sat back down. "Are you sure you wouldn't care for a coffee before you leave, dear?" she asked Solaina. Victoria's full composure slid back over her as if the last angry words had never been uttered. "Or a brandy perhaps?"

"Would have never what?" Howard asked, his voice growing calmer. His hands were shaking, though, and he was turning red.

Victoria glanced across the table at her husband, and what Solaina saw in her eyes was pure ice. Not that spark of love she'd always seen before. Not the one she'd counted on in the most perfect relationship she'd ever known. "Tried to stop you, darling. I wouldn't have tried to stop you."

"Dear God," Solaina gasped. "It was you?"

Victoria nodded demurely as she picked up her coffee-cup. "I never meant anyone any harm. I thought the first few incidents would serve as a warning, then David would scamper away and be done with that silly hospital nonsense. Which he didn't. And I really never meant for him to be so badly injured. That was a mistake because the man I made arrangements with was greedy for that vehicle David was driving. And I might add that I didn't pay the fellow after that. Not after what he did to poor David. He kept my pistol, too. My lovely little pearl-handled pistol. I do miss it. Howard gave it to me to protect myself from the snakes here, you know. It was so considerate of him to think of my safety when he was gone."

Across the table, Howard choked, then grabbed a glass of wine.

"And I do regret all that mess," Victoria continued. "Dreadfully."

Solaina glanced at Howard, who was speechless. "And the

hospital?" she asked, turning slowly back to Victoria. "You did that, too? You burned down David's hospital?"

"Not intentionally. I think there was a language problem. I instructed the man to start a fire in the storage room. One of the ones outside the building. I would have never…" Victoria choked, then dropped her head and started to sob quietly. "I would never have intentionally tried to hurt anyone. I just wanted my husband back, and I thought that since IMO didn't want him any more, and if David wasn't around to take up his time…I'm so sorry."

"Victoria!" Howard gasped, then fell sideways out of his chair onto the floor.

Without a word Solaina dashed around the table and dropped to her knees. As her fingers sought the pulse in his neck, she saw that he wasn't breathing. "Call an ambulance!" she choked, as she opened Howard's mouth to breathe into it.

No response.

So she gave him a thump in the chest, but that did not start his heart beating. Then, for the next ten minutes, waiting for the ambulance to arrive, Solaina intermittently pounded on Howard's chest, then breathed into his lungs, until help finally came and he was taken off to the hospital.

When Solaina followed the ambulance attendants out of the door, Victoria was still seated at the dining-room table, fussing to get the linen napkin placed properly in her lap and sipping her after-dinner coffee.

Alone.

"He's going to make it," David said, stepping out of the intensive care room. "His blood gases are improving and he's beginning to breathe better. They've decreased his oxygen. It's going to be rough, though. With his age… He's going to need quite a bit of cardiac rehab and I think he's going to have to go back to London to get it."

Solaina was slumped against the wall in the same spot she'd been for the past twelve hours. David had been there for the last six, mostly at Howard's bedside. "And after that?" she asked. "What is Howard supposed to do once he's recovered?"

David pulled off his gown and dropped it into the hamper next to the door, then walked across the hall and sat down on the bench next to Solaina. "One day at a time."

"One *lousy* day at a time."

"I'm not going to press charges," he said. "I don't think it would serve any purpose to send Victoria to prison. And what's done is done. With so many years together, maybe they can work something out for the ones they have left." He paused, smiling sadly. "I hope they can."

"I'm glad you're doing that," Solaina said, slipping her hand into his. "They've both got so much to get through now."

"Victoria's off in her own little world now. I talked to the authorities a while ago and they said she hadn't come round, that she just sits and stares."

"Waiting for the man she loves, I think." Solaina leaned her head against David's shoulder. She'd talked to him often since she'd left Vista. When she'd said goodbye, he hadn't protested, hadn't tried to convince her to stay. She'd simply said she had to go away and work it out on her own, and she'd asked him not to come after her. It had been so difficult, driving off that day, knowing how he needed her, but the Solaina who had gone away hadn't been the one he needed, or the one she'd wanted to be.

This was the first she'd seen him in all those months, and it felt very good. "I've missed you," she whispered. "Terribly."

"I've missed you, too."

She laughed. "You haven't been lurking about in the halls, watching me, as you did the first you saw me, have you?"

"Every time I get the urge, Matteo ties me up."

"It's nice, not having to worry about your ribs," she said, snuggling in even tighter.

"It's nice not having ribs that need to be worried about." He placed a light kiss on top of her head. "And I've missed the jasmine, pretty lady. I've taken to sleeping with a bar of your jasmine soap under my pillow."

Solaina laughed. "And I've planted a little rhododendron bush outside my window." She paused. "I called my father earlier, David."

"And?"

"And nothing. He was glad to know he's no longer under suspicion, even though the authorities never investigated him. And he still wants me to take over as administrator of IMO. Or as nurse administrator of a hospital he's affiliated with in Brazil. Nothing ever changes with him."

"It has with me," David said. "Although it took a whole hospital burning down for me to figure it out. And I'm sorry, Solaina. All the time I was insisting that you were something you insisted you were not I should have been listening to you. *Listening better.* And helping you get over your fears and doubts, instead of telling you they were silly. Which was what I was doing, you know."

"I know," she said softly.

"And all that *after* you'd told me how you'd spent a lifetime of being dictated to being told who you were and what you could or could not do."

"But I allowed it, David. I knew my inadequacies, and I

didn't do anything to fix them…to fix my life. Because it was easier. Then I saw all those people at Vista who had to start over…" She shook her head. "I've always blamed the tragedy with Jacob Renner as my excuse for not moving on, for not doing what I really wanted to do. It was a nice safe place to hide. A nice safe place to keep myself from not getting hurt again."

"And here I was, not listening to you, even though you kept telling me. But you've got to know that I never saw you as you saw yourself, Solaina. Never perceived your abilities as you did. Of course, I was hiding out in my own little world of denial, wasn't I? Because you're right. Sometimes it is easier. It makes us less vulnerable."

"Or more. And I didn't know how vulnerable I was until the night of the fire. I was in my element, directing the emergency scene, because that's what I do. But when you told me you needed me…" She paused, weighing her next words. "That scared me so much, David, because I wanted to be everything you needed. But I couldn't. And I don't even know if it was my lack of skills, or…" Solaina smiled demurely "…my perception of my lack, but I truly couldn't be what you wanted, even though I knew you loved me and would forgive me anything. Even forgive me if it turned out my father had been behind burning down the hospital. And, believe me, staying with you would have been so easy. But I couldn't. Not with you expecting something from me that I wasn't. It would have ruined us eventually because we don't have the luxury of separations in our life, David. Not like many people, where the professional life stops at the threshold before the personal one begins. For us, it carries over. One is the other. Professional is personal. And I truly didn't know if I could ever become all that you needed, David. I had to find me before I could be with you in every sense that we should be together, and you're the *only* person who has ever made me want to do that."

"I'm so sorry, Solaina. I was so caught up in loving you, and kicking myself for being bad at relationships, and not wanting to hurt you because I *was* so bad, that I was being horrible and hurting you in a way I didn't even understand."

"It wasn't you, and it wasn't me. It was what we'd allowed ourselves to become, I think. But we can't do that again," she said. "It's about listening, David. With the heart, but in a very unromantic and practical sense, with the ears, too."

"Even the most perfect relationships are difficult. I don't think Howard ever listened to Victoria, not with his ears anyway, and what he saw was his perception of their marriage."

"We all have our glitches, don't we? But I'm becoming a good nurse, David. I've moaned about it for all these years, and yet I've never done anything about it. One of my biggest glitches perhaps. I'm working at it, though. And I'm not shabby."

"So, toward the effort of listening better, which I promise to do, am I allowed to say that you're not shabby?"

Solaina laughed. "It's a start, isn't it?"

"I think Howard would testify to that. He was asking for you a while ago, by the way. Going on and on about the *not shabby* way you saved his life."

"Did he say anything about Victoria? Or ask about her?"

David shook his head. "I think he's still in a bit of shock. Maybe he doesn't fully realize what she's done. Or maybe he does, and there's nothing for him to say right now. But he loves her, and he'll get her through it."

"It's so sad, to love so fiercely and to feel so alone in it. I feel sorry for her, David. I know that's a terrible thing to say after everything she's done, but I do feel sorry for her. She was just trying to find a way to hold onto the man she loves."

"And you, pretty lady? Are you going to find a way to hold onto the man you love?"

Solaina pulled away from him, but didn't answer.

"I haven't bothered you about what you're doing at the hospital because I admire what you're doing, starting over. But you've got to know that I've been going crazy without you. And after what just happened with Howard and Victoria, we can't let this drag on, Solaina. Life's too short. We have to be together."

"I know that. But right now I still need more time, David, before I come back to Vista as a practicing nurse." *And anything else you have in mind.* "I am doing better, though. The dreams about Jacob Renner aren't as frequent…"

"You won't mind the bedpan brigade?"

"I'd love the bedpan brigade."

"And changing bed linen?"

"I'm getting especially good at bed linen. Nice square corners."

"And you wouldn't be averse to marrying the hospital director?"

"More than anything, I wouldn't be averse to marrying the hospital director. If the hospital director doesn't mind his wife doing bedpans and bed linen for a while."

"So, in the meantime, until you come home, can I sneak into the nurses' quarters at your clinic sometimes?" he asked, pulling her back into his arms.

"I'm counting on it. I need to have someone mess up that

bed linen so I can practice my square corners." A contented sigh escaped her lips. "I've always loved you, David. From that first crazy moment you asked me about my trees, I knew right then I wanted more than just an arboreal relationship with you."

He chuckled. "You never did tell me which you preferred. Evergreen or deciduous?"

"I'd prefer the one under which we could sit with our picnic hamper and pass the day making love on a blanket, I think." She kissed him softly on the lips, then laid her head against his chest. No more running. Not ever again. For the first time in her life Solaina Léandre had everything she needed. And wanted. Thank the *repaired,* smiling, red-lipped Buddha David had slipped into her hands earlier and she, in turn, had slipped onto the bed stand next to Howard. Howard's road was tough now, but she and David, and their Nirvana-gazing, red-lipped friend, would be there to help him through, as he'd done for them both.

"And permit me to say that my expectations of you under the tree are definitely not shabby."

"Care to come back to my little room and show me some of those expectations, Casanova?"

"Care to wear an orchid over your left ear, pretty lady?" he asked, handing her a small flower box.

"For the rest of my life."

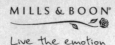

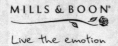

4 FREE

BOOKS AND A SURPRISE GIFT!

We would like to take this opportunity to thank you for reading this Mills & Boon® book by offering you the chance to take FOUR more specially selected titles from the Medical Romance™ series absolutely FREE! We're also making this offer to introduce you to the benefits of the Reader Service™—

- ★ **FREE home delivery**
- ★ **FREE gifts and competitions**
- ★ **FREE monthly Newsletter**
- ★ **Exclusive Reader Service offers**
- ★ **Books available before they're in the shops**

Accepting these FREE books and gift places you under no obligation to buy, you may cancel at any time, even after receiving your free shipment. Simply complete your details below and return the entire page to the address below. You don't even need a stamp!

YES! Please send me 4 free Medical Romance books and a surprise gift. I understand that unless you hear from me, I will receive 6 superb new titles every month for just £2.75 each, postage and packing free. I am under no obligation to purchase any books and may cancel my subscription at any time. The free books and gift will be mine to keep in any case.

M6ZED

Ms/Mrs/Miss/Mr ....Initials ....
                                                                    BLOCK CAPITALS PLEASE

Surname ....

Address ....

....

....Postcode...

Send this whole page to:
UK: FREEPOST CN81, Croydon, CR9 3WZ